The Ruin of Us

by

Keira Michelle Telford

www.venaticpress.com

"The only way to get rid of a temptation is to yield to it. Resist it, and your soul grows sick with longing for the things it has forbidden to itself."

-- Oscar Wilde
(from *The Picture of Dorian Gray*)

SHE CROSSED HER LEGS AT THE KNEE. MADDIE noticed that when Miss Camille first sauntered into her room and perched on the edge of her bed, asking questions about this and that, making small talk. Otherwise, she was the utmost picture of respectability.

She wore the finest navy blue silk dress. The black lace collar came up high on her neck, buttoned to her throat, and a silver chatelaine hung from her waist, the keys of the house affixed to it. In that way, she exuded refinement.

Her movements were fluid and graceful, and she walked with a practiced elegance, every step measured and precise. A pair of teardrop earrings set with sapphire gems swayed with the motion of her body. Were they real? They might well have been paste, but it didn't matter; that wasn't what people were looking at when their eyes fell upon her.

She had the softest face. Maddie swore her cheeks had the lightest dusting of rouge, her lips pinkened with tinted beeswax, but no-one would ever dare to suggest as much. Whatever tricks she employed to enhance her outward beauty—and to conceal the inevitable encroachment of age, for she must've been in her decline—were no business of anyone's.

Everyone loved her. She wasn't a schoolmistress as such, for the establishment she ran wasn't a school—not in the strictest sense. It was Miss Harper's House of Etiquette, and its function was to prepare blossoming young girls for society life and marriage. It was to provide the finishing touches, if you will. It was to make women out of girls: to strip them of the awkwardness of adolescence and prime them for their coming out. Among the better social classes, it was a well-regarded institute for molding wearisome teens into elegant debutantes, and Maddie was its latest inductee.

"I do believe you're the youngest girl we've ever welcomed here," Camille noted, her full lips curled into a warm smile. "You've only recently turned sixteen, yes?"

Maddie nodded. Less than a week had passed since her birthday celebrations, and she rather got the impression that her mother and father—if she were generous enough to call them that, which she seldom was—had been bursting to get rid of her. Not that she cared. In fact, gazing at Camille upon her bed, she felt a small splash of satisfaction. They'd not have sent her off quite so keenly if they knew the type of woman they were entrusting her to. The type of woman who crossed her legs at the knee.

"I hope you'll settle well with us." Camille's smile broadened. "Most girls do."

As she spoke, she tucked a wayward lock of honey-colored hair behind her ear, her waist-length tresses pinned up in a loose bun, several untamed blonde curls spilling out, framing her face and cascading down her neck. Some would've frowned upon her for that—after all, if one's hair is kept so brazenly unrestrained, what must that say of one's morals?—but Maddie thought such insouciance was daringly bohemian.

"Your parents have written to me warning that you might be somewhat resistant," Camille went on, casting an interested eye over the contents of Maddie's half-unpacked steamer trunk that lay open on the floor. "They've enjoined me to use a firm hand. Will that be necessary, do you think?"

Maddie lowered her gaze, glimpsing a splash of pale knit silk stockings above a pair of black leather ankle boots as her eyes fell from Camille's face to her feet.

With her legs crossed in such an outrageous manner, her skirts were drawn up a little, peaking several inches below the knee and exposing more than they ought. From within these many layered folds—silk upon cotton upon cotton upon silk—Maddie spied the embroidered lace hem of a silk petticoat. Her petticoat! The very garment that lay directly against her body!

Distracted by that thought, she was slow to respond to the question she'd been asked.

"I shan't cause you any bother," she said at last. "But I do not think I belong here."

"Why not?" Camille cocked her head inquiringly. "Simply because you weren't born to privilege?"

Maddie's mouth opened, but no sound made its way out. Camille's knowledge of her circumstance shocked her, for it was quite the usual course of things to pretend that her adoption had never occurred, as if she just appeared in her new family's bosom by magic. No-one ever made mention of her former life. Certainly not the part about the foundling home.

"Your provenance is of no consequence to me," Camille assured her, dismissing the past with a wave of her hand. "It saddens me to think that you consider yourself less deserving than the other girls. How you came to be in this world has no bearing on your character."

"But I don't fit," Maddie insisted. "I'm an orphan."

"So am I," Camille revealed without a hint of shame. "My mother died when I was fourteen, and I never knew my father." She clasped her hands over her knee and flexed her ankle, not seeming to care that it was on display. "A girl's position in life is not fixed, Madeline. She can be bettered."

Maddie cringed. "Please don't call me that."

"Is it not your name?" One of Camille's eyebrows arched toward the ceiling.

"It's what *they* call me." Maddie tried not to inject too much venom into her voice. "They are quite obstinate about it, but my real mother always called me by the diminutive: Maddie."

"Maddie," Camille repeated, testing the sound of it on her tongue. "You would prefer it if I called you this also?"

Her eyes were like the ocean: two deep pools of pale green flecked with gray and blue. They had a hypnotizing effect, and Maddie was entranced.

"Very much." The teen forced herself to look away and caught her rather wilted reflection in the mirror atop the vanity.

She looked tired. Her brunette mane—somewhat disheveled from the long train ride—was tumbling from a hasty up-sweep. Her cheeks were pink, not because they were rouged, or because the spring evening was particularly muggy, but because the temperature of the room had curiously risen several degrees since Camille walked in.

For want of something to keep her hands busy, lest she should fidget and pick at her nails—a vulgar habit, so said her adoptive mother—she resumed her halfhearted unpacking and plucked a small hatbox from her steamer trunk.

While attempting to set it out of the way on top of the armoire, she stood on her tippy toes, lifted it above her head, and felt a cool breeze tickle her underarms, her attention drawn to a distinct and inexplicable dampening there. Afraid that Camille might see the telltale wetness seeping into her dress and think her dirty, she dropped her arms, the hatbox still clasped in her hands.

"Can you not reach?" Camille rose from the bed and relieved her of it.

She was tall, Maddie realized then. Perhaps it was the French in her blood. Were French people particularly statuesque? She didn't know. Upon her arrival that morning, the other girls—only half a dozen in number—had taken great pleasure in feeding her snippets of Camille's history. Though most of it seemed mere conjecture, her French provenance was one of the few undisputed facts she'd managed to glean. Ergo, after the box had been successfully stashed away, she sought to impress her exotic new *maîtresse* by thanking her in poorly enunciated *français*.

"Murr-sea," she mumbled, not at all sure of the proper pronunciation.

Camille broke into an amused grin. "Someone's been talking about me, I see. How frightfully dangerous." Her eyes shimmered in the candlelight. "If those little gossipmongers tell you anything in the slightest bit unflattering, do ignore it." She winked.

As if there was any chance of that. In the few short hours Maddie had been at the house, she'd heard nothing but praise and fawning admiration for Camille:

She has the kindest heart and treats us all so well. She was born in Paris. Isn't that exotic, Maddie? Don't you think it is? She's an artist, you know. We all wish to be painted by her, if only she would ask. She always has a favorite to dote on. Perhaps this year it will be you!

In it all, no-one uttered a single ill thought, and throughout her grand tour of the building and grounds—which the girls whisked her away on directly she set foot in the place—Maddie soaked up every word. Long before evening fell, she was already enamored.

"I suppose I ought to let you get some sleep." Camille explored the few meager belongings Maddie had thus far unpacked and heaped in a disorderly pile atop the vanity. "You must be exhausted. It's been a long day."

She ran her fingers over the bust of a plain cotton nightgown flung hastily over a small bundle of books bound in silk ribbon and Maddie gasped. A paperback of the most erotic variety hid among the pile, and Camille was perilously close to uncovering it.

"You like to read?" She fished out the stack and scanned the titles. "Oh, my! This is some advanced literature indeed." A smile twitched at her lips.

Maddie hovered by the armoire, her buttocks tensed and ready for a lashing. "You must birch me now, I suppose."

"Must I?" Camille slipped the forbidden book from the bunch and flipped through its pages. "I rather think I should pretend I never saw it." She paused to read a few paragraphs, then handed it over. "Wouldn't that be preferable?"

Accepting it back into her possession, Maddie blushed. "Yes, thank you." Her fingers grazed Camille's. "I shan't read it again."

"What a shame that would be." Camille let the smile break free. "Books are to be read as a woman is to be loved: deeply and without restraint." She headed for the door. "Try not to stay up too late. Get some rest." She lingered at the threshold of the room. "Goodnight, Maddie."

From that moment on, Maddie had but one aim: she wanted to be Camille's favorite.

IN THE ENSUING WEEKS, MADDIE STROVE TO BE
noticed by Camille. Though she didn't care one
bit for improving herself for purpose of ensnaring
a husband, she did all that she could to excel in
whatever endeavor Camille set to her, whether it
was needlework, dancing, or the reading of
poetry—all of which she hated in equal measure.

Dance lessons were particularly tedious.
Camille's focus invariably centered on the girls
who required the most coaching, while Maddie's
focus was on her derrière, admiring how the
ruffles and pleats of her skirts fell over her rump,
enhancing its shape. It never occurred to her that
the ballroom was lined with mirrors, and that
Camille could quite easily see where her
attentions were fixed. And it certainly never
occurred to her that she might like it.

Proficient in many forms of dance, including
the polka, the schottische, and the waltz, Camille
always led, and she seemed perfectly at ease in
the role. Persistent but unsubstantiated rumors

that she also knew how to cancan—a scandalous talent no doubt learnt in Paris—were repeatedly brushed off with a good-natured laugh, but Maddie believed every word and had no difficulty imagining it. Indeed, those tantalizing daydreams significantly alleviated the monotony of watching her peers fumble all over the ballroom.

"Look at me, not at your feet," Camille reminded the hopelessly clumsy girl in her arms, frustration seeping into her voice. "It's unattractive."

When the girl finally did succeed in keeping her head up, everything else fell apart. She stepped forward when she ought to have stepped back, bumped Camille's chest, trampled one of her boots underfoot, and trod hard on her toe.

"You really do have the most dreadful coordination," Camille grumbled, calling an abrupt halt to the dance. "It's a wonder to me that you haven't yet caused someone an injury."

She looked over the rest of the group, making her next selection, and Maddie's heart thrummed when their eyes met.

"Your turn." Camille bent forward and held her hand out, playing the role of the gentleman. "Will you favor me with your hand for this dance?"

Gladly! Oh, so gladly, Maddie thought as the rest of the world melted away and Camille drew her to the middle of the ballroom floor.

"You've been watching me closely, I hope." Camille led them in a waltz. "You always do."

Determined not to err as the previous girl had done, Maddie fixed her eyes upon Camille's. She wouldn't look down—not even for a second—

14

but Camille did. Her gaze broke away for a moment and dropped to Maddie's lips. Her lips! She corrected the mistake immediately, but not without a slight blush coloring her cheeks.

Maddie had never been kissed, but she'd read about it in books. Always, there seemed to be the moment before the kiss where one looked to the other's mouth, as if in contemplation of intimacy. Did Camille want to kiss her? Maddie chastised herself for the foolish thought as soon as it fluttered into her mind and concentrated instead on her steps. She'd been taught to dance, but was mechanical about the operation. Emotionless. Dispassionate.

"You're too stiff." Camille took her by the shoulders and gave her a little shake, loosening her up. "Dancing is a prelude, yes? Good dancers make good lovers."

Giggles erupted at the sidelines.

Ignoring them, Camille slid her hand onto Maddie's lower back, resting it above her rump. "Our bodies must work together, as though we were—" She stopped herself and lowered her voice. "More intimately entwined." She took Maddie's hand in hers and coached her. "Your movements must be sympathetic to mine. Feel the motion of my body and respond accordingly."

Maddie had no trouble at all with that. What she had considerable difficulty with was remaining at an appropriate distance. When Camille took a strong step forward, she took a small step back, relaxing her elbows so that Camille was drawn incrementally closer.

"You're standing much too near," Camille warned as their bosoms brushed together. "If you're not careful, we shall soon be in a full embrace." She separated their bodies, enforcing propriety, and they continued to waltz.

Throughout, Maddie's head swirled, her nostrils filled with the scent of Camille's exotic French perfume. Her palm grew clammy in Camille's hand, though it was only grasped softly, Camille's touch featherlight. Her breathing grew heavy. She became dizzy, stumbled over her own feet, and crumpled against Camille's chest, saved from plummeting to the parquet floor only by Camille's quick action.

"That's enough for today." Camille took hold of her waist, keeping her upright. "Who's for some tea and biscuits?"

As SPRING ROLLED INTO SUMMER, THE HEAT became unbearable. Many lessons were moved outside, but poetry reading always took place in the stuffy and ill-ventilated library. For relief, Camille often threw open the tiny windows and perched upon the nearby desk, maximizing her exposure to whatever breeze came drifting through. When that wasn't enough, she'd unfasten the top buttons of her bodice.

In her characteristically risqué manner, she'd ease the high lace collar away from her lily white skin and tilt her head, letting the cool air kiss her neck. Once, Maddie saw her fish a large chip of ice from a pitcher of water. She held it just below her ear and let it melt there, sighing as tiny rivulets of the cool liquid cascaded downward, trickling over her exposed collarbone and disappearing under her clothing.

At the end of these most sweltering days, when all the girls were shifting uncomfortably in their drawers, their backs slick with sweat, their inner thighs clammy, Camille would spring from the desk and declare that a trip to the lake was in order.

Nestled at the heart of the house's expansive gardens, the lake was a private refuge for the girls during the excruciatingly hot summer months. Camille never swam in it—not that anyone ever saw—but she always sat near the water's edge, supervising the proceedings while reclined on a blanket beneath the shade of a large oak.

Since the girls didn't have bathing suits, they swam in their shemmies. Quite without inhibition, they ran to the bank of the lake and stripped off to their undergarments. The most demure girls went in with their drawers on, but the additional layer afforded them little more modesty. When saturated with water, the thin cotton became disgracefully translucent. But what did it matter? There was no-one there to see. No-one except Camille.

As they splashed and squealed and frolicked, Camille watched. As they emerged from the water, cotton clinging to skin, she watched. As they chased each other along the little wooden jetty and leapt into the very deepest part of the lake, she watched.

Many of them were enviably well-formed. Their full, youthful bosoms bounced and jiggled, their nipples stiffened by the chill of the water. Where their uppermost thighs came together, there was the dark shadow of womanly bloom— something which Maddie had only just begun to appreciate on her own body.

Having spent her early childhood poor, with little in the way of decent meals, the pleasantly curvaceous figure she'd developed in recent years

18

still felt alien to her. She had little confidence in it, and so lingered at the lakeside, hesitant to join in.

"Whatever's the matter?" Camille inquired of her. "Can you not swim?"

Maddie nodded. She learnt to swim in the public baths.

"Then what is it?" Camille persisted. "Do you not wish to cool off?"

Maddie did, and yet she remained at the edge of Camille's blanket, her knees tucked to her chest. "Will you watch me?" she asked at last, toying with the top button of her bodice.

"If you want me to." Camille eyed that button intently. "I shan't take my eyes off you, I promise."

That assurance was all Maddie needed to hear. She fumbled with her bodice and cast it off with her camisole, then wriggled out of her skirts. Her corset was abandoned next, followed by her boots and stockings. She considered keeping on her drawers, but thought better of it when she saw how keenly Camille's eyes followed the girls who didn't. Though her hands were trembling, she unfastened the waist drawstring and let them drop to the ground, then scampered to the lake and submerged herself in it.

Knowing full well what immediate effect the water would have on her white shemmy, she surfaced facing Camille and awaited her appraisal—which came in the form of a kiss. Camille pressed one to her fingertips and blew it in her direction, then settled back against the tree with a broad, satisfied smile on her lips.

SATURDAY EVENINGS WERE RESERVED FOR GLASSES of warm sweetened milk, biscuits, and classic literature. The girls would gather around, jostling for position as Camille settled in an armchair in the parlor and read to them, pausing at intervals to quiz them on the text, assessing their comprehension of the subject matter.

All but Maddie clamored to win favor. While her peers vied to be the first to answer any questions Camille posed, her participation dwindled as she became ever more absorbed in other pursuits. Whenever possible, she assumed a spot beside the arm of Camille's chair, sitting at her feet like a loyal puppy. From that vantage point, she had a perfect view of Camille's boot-clad ankles and was often lucky enough to espy a flash of stocking.

Attempting to do so without being caught, she'd rove her eyes up and down Camille's skirts, looking for the telltale line of her garter. How high did her stockings go? Did she garter above the knee or below? As a child, Maddie gartered below the knee. Most girls of her class did, but as she grew older and found herself in better company, her garters were raised a few inches above her knee, as was more befitting of her new position in life.

Sadly, Camille's garter line was well concealed beneath multiple layers of flounced silk. For all the hours Maddie spent with her eyes pinned to Camille's thighs, she caught not the faintest glimpse of it, but her fascination did not go unnoticed.

After every reading, Camille held one of the girls back to help her straighten the room before bed. Empty glasses must be gathered up. Crumbs must be swept away. Cushions and blankets must be returned to their rightful places. To be fair about the business, she rotated through the small group in alphabetical order, and Maddie waited with mounting impatience for her next turn: another chance to be alone with Camille.

She loved the way Camille moved about the room, humming to herself as she beat the indentations of adolescent buttocks out of the cushions and shook biscuit remnants from the folds of the blankets, her skirts swishing about her ankles. They often talked. Camille regaled her with stories from her past, and once, under the guise of extra practice, they waltzed in front of the hearth.

It was an unhurried, intimate dance, and in the privacy of the parlor, Camille made no objection when Maddie stood too close. In fact, Maddie was certain that she tightened her grip.

"You're such a beautiful girl." Camille harnessed her firmly by the waist and drew her near, their flushed faces illuminated by the candles on the mantel. "You're a good learner, too—intelligent and quick-witted—but you've been quiet these past few weeks. Is there something wrong?"

Maddie shook her head. As time went on, she found words increasingly difficult to come by in Camille's presence.

"You've been distracted during our readings," Camille continued, their dance slowing. "Is this what you've been looking for?" She halted them, brought Maddie's hand to her hip and nudged it down, letting it glide over her body. "Does this satisfy your curiosity?"

She pressed the teen's palm firmly to her outer thigh, and there, a few inches above her knee, was the telltale ridge of an elastic garter.

Maddie couldn't breathe. Her breath was trapped in her lungs, her mouth agape. She wanted to freeze that moment in time—capture it forever, as in a photograph—but it was shattered in an instant. At the sound of footsteps in the hall—likely the housemaid coming down to begin her evening chores—Camille slapped her hand away and withdrew.

"Off you go to bed now." She dismissed her dumbstruck charge. "I shall see you in the morning, bright and early for church."

That should've been enough. Maddie should've been delighted with that single moment of stolen impropriety and never have expected anything more, but the very next time Camille called her name, she was determined that there should be a repeat of the indiscretion. Preferably one without the interruption of the maid. Indeed, she felt so sure of it that when the

23

glasses were cleared away, the crumbs were swept, and the cushions and blankets were tidied, she failed to depart. Camille bade her an abrupt goodnight, but she stayed put.

"Is there something on your mind?" Camille kept to a reserved distance. "If there is, do spit it out. I haven't the patience for guessing games."

Maddie edged closer and extended a hand. "May I feel it again?"

Camille suppressed a shiver and laughed. "Whatever for? Don't be silly."

If she'd been more astute, Maddie would've seen the pain etched on Camille's brow at the moment of rejection. She would've seen the furrows of tension that puckered her unblemished forehead, and heard that her laugh was hollow. She would've noticed how Camille turned her back, not to show callous indifference, but to obscure the welling of tears in her eyes. Instead, feeling disparaged, she hung her head and slunk from the room.

ONCE A WEEK, CAMILLE TOOK THE GIRLS ON AN outing. Whether she opted for the nearest beach, the zoo, or a noisy London music hall, there was always some event that necessitated a good deal of primping and preening and dressing in one's Sunday best. Of course, regardless of the destination, the highlight for Maddie was in competing for the much coveted spot beside Camille on the train.

She rarely succeeded—the other girls were much too boisterous—but every time she got beaten to the post, Camille flashed her a sympathetic smile. Somehow, that made the loss more bearable. The acknowledgement of her struggles fueled her determination—no matter if it conveyed shared disappointment, as she hoped, or merely pity—and late one evening, after they nearly missed the last train back to the house and everyone was in a state of fatigue, she finally shoved her way into the passenger carriage ahead of the pack.

25

That night, Camille sat by the window, fanning herself with a folded playbill. The air was particularly stale and stuffy, and as Maddie shifted on the padded leather seat, trying to get comfortable, she noticed Camille's dainty ungloved hand resting between them, inviting touch. Not that she had the temerity to solicit contact. Fearing another rejection, she feigned nonchalance and laid her own hand there, inches away. It felt dangerous, but a quick glance around the carriage assured her that the other girls were oblivious. Most were sleeping and the rest were trying to.

Though she knew she was trespassing, she crept her hand across the divide until the tip of her little finger grazed Camille's. She expected nothing. Convinced that her attentions were unwanted, she waited to be pushed away. Instead, she felt a warmth. Camille's hand slid over hers, plucked it from the seat, and whisked it onto her lap, laying it directly over her garter.

Maddie stifled a whimper. She had no right to touch Camille in such a way, yet as she roamed her greedy hand over the garter, feeling above and below it, Camille seemed in no hurry to rob her of the experience. In fact, the stoic older woman never gave any indication that anything untoward was taking place, nor that she was at all affected by it. Throughout, she remained gazing at the passing countryside, even though complete darkness blanketed the scenery and there was nothing whatever to see.

Exploiting her unusually permissive mood, Maddie chanced more. Without warning, she helped herself to Camille's hand and placed it on her own thigh, over her own garter, urging reciprocal intimacy, and she thought she heard a gasp.

At first, Camille's hand lay limp, as if in shock. Seconds ticked by, then it moved. Camille's thumb brushed her garter, then the whole hand squeezed. As a beam of moonlight hit her face, Maddie saw that her eyes were closed. She caught her lower lip between her teeth and swallowed hard, but was too soon jolted back to her senses when the train slowed at the next station. One of the other girls stirred and her hand drifted away, the heat lost.

Never a word was spoken, and a full week of uninterrupted tedium—and scrupulously, infuriatingly good behavior—passed before Maddie had another spectacular chance to become more intimately acquainted with Camille's garters. Indeed, it was gloriously unexpected, for the evening of their next excursion began fraught with unpleasant tension.

In a glaring deviation from the norm, Maddie made no bid to secure the seat beside Camille on the outward bound train journey. She had a plan. Having concluded that there was little chance of any inappropriateness taking place when the other girls were all so wired for a night out at a London theater, she opted to reserve her efforts for the return trip, but the unintentional slight had a strong and immediate effect.

Rather than the usual pained smile from Camille, a flutter of confusion etched itself on her brow. Her naturally full lips seemed tight, her mouth small and taut, and she fell peculiarly quiet, barely saying a nice word to anyone until she lubricated her good spirits with a little booze during the first intermission.

Champagne was her drink of choice that night. She bought each of the girls a glass, which brought on giggles aplenty, but Maddie felt sure it all went straight to her bladder. Needing to relieve herself, she broke from the group to use the lavatory, which was simply a small room with a single private stall, a washbasin, and a padded chair on which to sit and wait. She heard someone enter behind her, but thought little of it until she'd seen to her necessaries, emerged from the stall, and found Camille standing by the washbasin.

She had one foot propped on the seat of the chair, her sapphire skirts hoisted over her knee, the hem of her petticoat on display, her leg bared beyond the top of one ungartered black stocking. Her whole leg, from ankle to ...

"I've had a frightful mishap." She dangled a broken garter in the air. "Do you have anything I might use to spare my dignity?"

Her mouth too dry to answer, Maddie jerked her eyes away. She had nothing in her pockets but a few mint humbugs and a hanky, but her hair was bound with red satin ribbons. Thinking one of them would suffice as a makeshift garter, she unraveled it from her up-do.

"Ah, yes! That will work! Might I borrow it?" Camille held out her hand.

Maddie wiped her suddenly clammy palms off on her dress and walked the ribbon over to Camille, trading it for the snapped garter: a limp strip of black elastic decorated with ruffled black satin and lace. Strangely, upon closer inspection, the garter did not appear frayed or worn. The break looked clean, is if it had met with the blade of a pair of sewing scissors.

"You may dispose of that." Camille closed Maddie's hand around the broken garter, then fastened the red ribbon in a bow around her thigh, securing her stocking in place. "There." She admired her handiwork. "Will that suit the purpose for now, do you think?"

In the grip of some unprecedented impulse, her head whirling with the possibility that Camille might've purposely engineered the failure of her garter, Maddie bent forward and pressed her lips to the splash of alabaster thigh above Camille's stocking.

Rendered momentarily speechless, Camille's eyes widencd and she drew a sharp breath, but made no objection to the gesture. Nor did she make any attempt to cover herself.

"Maddie," she whispered. "My darling ..."

At the sound of her name, Maddie leapt back, deeply embarrassed by her impudence. "I'm so sorry!" She shuffled away in disgrace, pocketing the broken garter. "I'm sure I don't know what I'm about!"

From then on, Maddie kept her distance. Even when she knew Camille was trying to solicit her company, she remained withdrawn. Until the day she received a most unwelcome letter from her parents. That day changed everything.

WELL AFTER LIGHTS OUT, MADDIE KNOCKED frantically upon the door to Camille's study. She'd been ignoring her parents' letters for several weeks, and had a stack of them heaped on her vanity. When she eventually decided to open them before bed, the news she found therein induced instant panic.

She knocked again.

Camille responded hastily to the second round of harried knocking, her bodice and under-bodice unfastened down to her bust, exposing her corset and the chemise beneath. "Whatever is it? What's wrong?"

Maddie couldn't answer. Her attention was immediately diverted from her troubles by the sight of Camille's lace-trimmed blue satin corset, the prominent bust gores embroidered with intricate loops and swirls. Oh, those bust gores ...

"Forgive me." Camille followed the trajectory of her eyes. "I wasn't expecting to be disturbed." She clasped her bodice together. "What is it that you need?"

As much as she tried, she couldn't conceal her undergarments, and as much as Maddie tried, she couldn't raise her eyes.

"For heaven's sake, do come inside before the maid happens by and sees you gawping." Camille released her bodice and pulled Maddie into her private candlelit sanctuary. "What is it that causes you to seek my company so late? You ought to be in bed."

"They intend for me to marry him," Maddie wailed, grief returning to her as she waved the offending letter at Camille. "What am I to do?"

"Marry whom?" Camille plucked the letter from the air and pored over its contents.

"I've never even met the boy," Maddie cried. "And nor do I wish to! If they make me go through with it, I shall refuse the business." She folded her arms defiantly. "I shall run away. It will have to be annulled, for I will *not* give myself up to him."

"Sshhh." Camille petitioned her to lower her voice. "Sit." She led her to the sofa. "You have been sent to me to prepare you for marriage. You know this, yes?" She retrieved a half-consumed glass of brandy from her desk. "Such a letter cannot have come as a surprise."

"But I do not wish to marry," Maddie declared boldly. "I think I should wither and die if I were confined as a wife."

"I understand your predicament." Camille sat beside her, brandy in hand. "Perhaps better than anyone."

"Then tell me," Maddie implored her. "What am I to do?"

"You are to do what we all must do," Camille answered solemnly, but honestly. "Enjoy what little freedom you have, while you still have it."

To Maddie's ears, that didn't sound much of a solution. "Why must I do as they please? Why can't I be like you? You have a fine life, and you're unbound by any man."

"Not by a man, that's true. But I am bound just as severely by many other things." Camille sipped her brandy. "As I'm sure you're already well aware, it can be inordinately difficult for a woman to obtain that which she truly wants." She touched a corner of the letter to the flame of a candle set on the table beside the sofa and watched it burn. "Very often, it is the prudent thing to accept a circumstance that's far from our ideal. In the end, it's a matter of survival." When the flames got too close to her fingers, she flicked the letter into an empty coal scuttle beside the hearth.

"What of love?" Maddie scooted closer, their knees touching.

"Love is the harshest master of them all." Camille allowed her to advance. "One is never more a prisoner than when in love." Her voice almost cracked. "Perhaps you might grow to love this boy."

"Could *you*?" Maddie pulled a face. "Could you grow to love a man?"

Camille downed the rest of her drink and set her empty glass aside. "No." She eased back into the cushions. "I'm not suited to marriage."

"Neither am I." Maddie burst into a fit of tears. "Don't you see that?"

She lunged forward, and Camille welcomed the distraught teen to her breast.

33

"Hush now." She held Maddie to her bosom. "Calm yourself."

That proved impossible, and Maddie sobbed heartily until she fell asleep in Camille's comforting arms. When she awoke some hours later, she found herself wilted against Camille's chest, her face pressed to the older woman's tear-dampened décolletage.

They were lying next to each other on the sofa, Camille half-reclined against the cushions, her head propped on her arm, and as Maddie pulled away, her gaze was snared once again by Camille's escaping bosom. Seeing no harm in feasting her eyes, since Camille appeared to be in a deep slumber, she peeled back Camille's open bodice, exposing the upper swells of her generous, tightly constrained breasts, admiring how they heaved with each breath.

Feeling brave, she laid her hand on one of the bust gores, the rigid, steam-molded fabric protecting Camille's chest like a plate of steel armor. Dissatisfied with that, she then ever so lightly tickled a finger from Camille's neck to her cleavage and dropped a kiss there.

One kiss.

Two.

Three ...

She peppered Camille's skin with a flurry of soft kisses and laid a hand on her thigh, feeling again that sacred place where she gartered. Oh, to see it once more! She pinched the hems of Camille's skirts between her fingers and raised them an inch. Only an inch.

Barely breathing, she paused, made sure Camille was at no risk of waking, then revealed more, baring the tops of her boots and her shins.

It was too much. Fearing that Camille might stir and realize she'd been molested, Maddie backed off the sofa and scurried away.

Once alone, Camille opened her eyes. She didn't wake, for she'd never been asleep. She merely opened her eyes and sighed, her skin tingling with the memory of Maddie's kisses.

SUNDAYS WERE A DAY OF RELAXATION. ALL THE girls were required to attend church, but after that, the day was theirs to do with as they wished. For everyone except Maddie, that meant gathering by the back fence and making eyes at Frederick, the local delivery boy.

Due to the house's rural location, close encounters with boys were a rarity. In fact, eighteen-year-old Frederick happened to be the only boy who had any legitimate cause to visit the house at all, and so drew an overwhelming amount of admiration. But not from Maddie.

Bored and lonely, Maddie routinely skulked about the house in search of something to amuse her. Sometimes, she'd bake a cake with the cook. Other times, she'd pick a book from the library and settle down to read. The house just wasn't the same without Camille in it, and on Sundays, Camille usually went out.

It was expected that she'd leave in the early afternoon to visit friends in London—or so the other girls supposed. She'd frequently be gone well into the evening, returning on the last train, and Maddie would lie in bed listening as she ascended the stairs after midnight, singing softly to herself. Wherever she went, she clearly had fun.

Her absence was so typical that to one day see her lounging on a blanket in the garden, enjoying a few moments of solitude under a parasol with a book, caught Maddie quite by surprise. Keen not to waste such an unexpected opportunity, she hurried out and hovered nearby, not presuming to invade Camille's privacy until she was invited to do so.

"You may sit." Camille looked up over her book. "I take it you do not wish to gawk at poor Frederick?" She quirked a lopsided, playful smile.

Maddie knelt on the edge of the blanket. "I'm not like the other girls in that way."

"I've noticed." Camille lowered the dog-eared paperback to her lap. "You are like me, perhaps. Your eye is caught by other attractions."

She wasn't wearing her boots, and as she said that, she drew one leg up so that her petite stockinged foot grazed the calf of her other leg and rumpled the hem of her skirts around her shins, baring herself almost to the knees. It was a rare and delicious sight, but Maddie forced herself not to stare.

"Are you unwell?" she wondered, worrying the folds in her satin skirts with the tips of her restless fingers. "Is that why you've remained at the house today?"

"Not unwell as such." Camille laid a hand on her abdomen, her manicured nails freshly buffed and colored pink. "I am afflicted with the onset of my monthlies, that is all. It's nothing to fret over. A little drop of laudanum does wonders for the discomfort."

In her naivety, Maddie wasn't entirely sure why the commencement of Camille's poorliness ought to prevent her from socializing with friends, but rather than fixate on the matter, she changed the subject.

"What are you reading?"

"Something you might appreciate." Camille passed the book over.

The title being unknown to her, Maddie read a few paragraphs, shocked to discover that it was the most explicit narrative of intimate love that she'd ever cast her inexperienced eyes upon. Not only that, but men didn't feature anywhere within its salacious pages.

"You like it?" Camille watched her cheeks color up. "You may borrow it if you wish, but you must promise me that it will remain our little secret."

Her passions stirred by the erotic text, Maddie discarded the novel and dove for one of Camille's feet. "Oh, Miss Camille! I want you so!" She crushed her lips to the woven silk encasing the delicate extremity and worked her kisses from the arch to the ankle to the shin, holding the limb reverently, cupping it in her palms like some precious artifact.

"My dear girl!" Camille recoiled from her grasp. "Where's your sense? Whatever's got into you?!" She glanced around, making sure the spontaneous display of worship wasn't witnessed by any of the other girls. Or worse, the maid. "You must control yourself. We could be seen!"

Suitably reprimanded, Maddie blurted a few mumbled apologies, rose from the blanket, and ran into the house, her vision blurred with tears. How could she ever look at Camille again? How could Camille possibly bear to be near her after she'd embarrassed herself to such a degree? Resolving to leave the place immediately, she bolted to her room, dragged her steamer trunk out from under the bed, and began throwing her clothes into it. Not a minute later, Camille breezed in.

"What in heaven's name are you doing?" She closed the door quietly behind her. "You surely do not intend to run away? Unpack your things at once. I've no wish for you to leave." She sounded uncharacteristically stern.

"How can I remain?" Maddie slumped on the bed, wiping her wet cheeks on her sleeves. "I've offended you so dreadfully."

"Offended me?" Camille sat beside her and took a firm hold of her hands. "My darling, you've done no such thing."

"But—"

"Listen to me." She pulled Maddie's hands into her lap. "I know well what you're feeling—believe me, I do. I am not offended by your passionate nature. Indeed, I am rather dangerously flattered by it." She raised Maddie's hands to her lips and kissed each finger in turn.

"You aren't cross with me?" Maddie sniffled.

"Not a bit." Camille shuffled closer. "But what you want from me, you cannot have." She looked pained. "I am not free to give it."

"You're under no vow." Maddie failed to see the problem, there being no husband to whom she must be loyal.

"That is not my bind." Camille refused to give way. "Now I shall not discourage you from looking at me as you do—I am too weak for that—but if you wish to kiss me again, you must make every effort to quell the impulse."

"How?"

"Think of how much damage could be done." Camille implored her to see reason. "Imagine what harm could come to you or I if your parents were to learn that I'd behaved improperly with you."

With a groan of frustration, Maddie tore her hands away from Camille and flopped onto her back. "But I am wound to such a fevered pitch."

"Then you must relieve the pressure." Camille addressed the problem with absolute pragmatism. "Bring a hand to yourself if that is what it takes."

Maddie's eyes widened. "You can't truly mean ... ?"

"You must," Camille insisted. "Whenever these feelings have a hold on you, you must abate them, as must I, else we shall both become delirious with want of it."

"I haven't a clue how such a thing is to be done," Maddie confessed. "I've never ..."

"Then I shall show you." Camille leant over her. "Close your eyes."

Maddie did as she was told, lying tame and passive as Camille raised her skirts and spread her untouched thighs.

"Use your fingers here." Camille guided Maddie's trembling fingertips through the overlapping split in her cotton drawers and to her saturated sex. "Wish that they were mine. The very thought will guide you to that precious peak."

Maddie howled and clutched at Camille's shoulder. The delightful pressures she felt then were unlike anything she'd ever known. Camille's undoubtedly expert touch directed the operation most precisely, teaching her to tickle, pinch, and rub all the critical parts so that, in only a few short minutes, her body stiffened.

"That's it, my darling." Camille coaxed her pleasure to crest. "Come for me."

Maddie held her mouth open, but no sound escaped. She arched her back and her thighs quivered, her insides pulsing. In seconds, it was over, the crisis passed.

"There now." Camille withdrew. "You are sated." Her lips brushed Maddie's forehead, and then she was gone, leaving Maddie in a flustered heap upon the bed.

THE FOLLOWING WEEKS PASSED EASILY. MADDIE counted every smile, her heart lifting each time Camille's eyes met hers. When there was little risk of being caught, there were light touches, furtive glances, and twice they danced alone in the parlor.

"You have such an exquisite figure," Camille praised her as they waltzed. "It's a true delight to have you in my arms."

Maddie yearned for more, but was always disappointed by Camille's resolute stance on the limitations of their closeness. Until the night she wasn't.

One Sunday night, Maddie—lying in bed, reading by candlelight—heard Camille's midnight footfalls on the staircase. They reached the landing, retreated some way down the hall, stopped, hesitated, and returned. They grew louder as they approached her bedroom door, then halted. Would she change her mind? Would she walk away?

Maddie waited with bated breath.

After an agonizing silence, there came a knock so faint that it could well have been mistaken for the old house's nightly protests against the wind, or the contracting of the aged wood as it cooled from the day's heat. Then the door opened a crack.

"May I come in?"

"Please." Maddie slid her book onto the nightstand and pulled the bedcovers up to her shoulders. She'd taken to sleeping in her chemise on the most sultry nights, since it was a much lighter garment than her nightgown, and she felt obscenely exposed.

"Are you shy?" Camille closed the door and approached the bed, the deep neckline of her red silk and velvet gown displaying her ample charms.

Maddie had never seen her in proper eveningwear before. She blushed at the sight and let the covers fall away from her shoulders. "If you wish to look at me, you may do so, though I haven't nearly as much to show."

Camille's rapt gaze fell to her chest. "I thought I ought to check on you." That weak excuse—no doubt conceived moments earlier in the hallway—was the only explanation she offered for her late night visitation. "How have you been feeling these past weeks?" She alighted on the edge of the bed. "You are much more contented in things now, I hope."

Maddie nodded. "To some degree."

"Only some?" Camille raised a perfectly tweezed eyebrow.

Maddie shrugged. "It pains me often. Some days, I feel I simply must kiss you else I might die for want of it. You walk by me in the hall and your presence chokes my breath. My heart pounds so heavy I feel it might burst."

"Oh, my darling." Camille scooted closer. "I do not wish for you to be made unwell by these passions." She leant forward and kissed the top of Maddie's head. "Have you been tending to yourself as I taught you?"

"Every morning and night." Maddie exaggerated only a little.

"And does it not relieve the ache?" Camille moved closer still.

Maddie smelt liquor on her breath and suspected that, in her noticeably elevated state, she might well be incapable of maintaining the moral fortitude she'd taken so much care to nurture during the course of their chaste flirtations. On the heels of that suspicion, the seeds of a mischievous notion took root.

"A little," she answered coyly. "But no pleasure since has ever compared to the pleasure I achieved when you were here with me." She paused, preparing to take advantage of Camille's impaired judgment. "Perhaps if you stayed awhile tonight, so that I might look upon you and feel you near me in the midst of the endeavor, my relief may be greatly enhanced."

It was a bold move—bolder than she'd ever been before—and she punctuated the suggestion by letting the covers slip further from her body, baring the full outline of her breasts to Camille's freely wandering eyes, her nipples stiffening directly.

"Will you watch me?" She wriggled onto her back, posing the question just as she had that first time at the lake—and every time thereafter.

It had become a private ritual between them. Before removing her clothes, she'd turn to Camille and ask, always receiving the same affirmative response. And true to her word, Camille never once looked away. It was as though the other girls were no longer there; they faded into the background while she stood in the fore.

"Will you?" Maddie urged her. "Like you do when I swim."

"If you want me to." Camille gave way, hitched up her skirts, and maneuvered onto the bed. "I shan't take my eyes off you, I promise." Her breathing quickened as she eased the covers down to Maddie's thighs. "Do it for me just this once. Give yourself a pleasure."

In a flash, Maddie's hand disappeared under her chemise. She teased the needy flesh of her most feminine parts with the tips of her fingers, and the room filled with her sensual sighs, the air thick with the perfume of her arousal.

"How does it feel?" Camille gazed on.

"It's gushing." Maddie whimpered. "It always does when I think of you."

"Let me see." With a visible tremor in her hand, Camille pinched the hem of Maddie's chemise between her fingers and inched it up, bunching it over her belly. "That's it, darling." She cast her eyes directly on the operation and saw the first shiver of impending climax ripple through Maddie's young body. "You're close now." She laid a hand on the teen's naked thigh, opening her wider, causing the petals of her glistening sex to bloom.

Maddie's hand worked feverishly. "Oh, it comes! It comes!" She threw her head back, her paroxysm erupting with a profusion of amatory juices, Camille's name whispered on her lips.

When it was over, she rolled onto her side and buried her face in Camille's décolletage, dropping a flurry of kisses on the upper swells of her confined breasts. "Thank you, thank you, thank you," she whispered, her voice muffled in the older woman's bosom.

Enervated by the intensity of her crisis, she lay still, recovering her breath. The hand that'd presently been employed in the most delicious of pursuits rested limply on the seat of her womanhood, her wetted fingers draped over the rich thicket of dark hair adorning her motte. She saw no reason to cover herself.

In a moment of weakness, Camille snatched up that hand. She smelt the musk of Maddie's sex and sucked those fingers into her mouth, devouring every drop of the precious dew that clung to them. "You taste divine."

She tried to get up then, but Maddie held on.

"Stay," the teen begged, gripping her waist. "A little longer. Please!"

"I cannot." Camille pried her arms away. "I dare not." She clambered off the bed with as much grace as she could muster in her rather inebriated condition. "I must retire."

Before she could get too far away, Maddie lunged for her. "Whatever you feel for me, do not regret this in the morning." She flung her arms around Camille's middle. "I should hate myself for it if you did."

"My darling, I regret it already." Camille extricated herself from Maddie's clutches once more. "But I'm afraid I would do it again just as fast." She cupped the teen's cheeks, tilted her head up, and pecked the tip of her nose. "Sleep well, my sweet angel."

With that, she slipped away, retreated to her own room, and collapsed upon the bed. Lacking the patience to undress, she drew her knees up, brought a hand to her saturated core, and gave herself the most intense spend, biting down on her lower lip to stifle a series of lewd cries that threatened to rouse the whole house. In the wake of it, she lay in the dark, panting.

MADDIE WAS RACKED WITH GUILT. SHE'D TEMPTED Camille when her faculties were not at full strength, knowing that she lacked the ability to resist. It was a wicked thing to have done, and now she, too, had regrets. The very thought that Camille, in the sober light of day, might look upon the memory of that night with anything short of sheer contented bliss made her sick to the pit of her stomach.

At a loss as to how she might properly apologize for her selfish behavior, she penned Camille a heartfelt note and slipped it into her study one night. Nothing short of a love letter, the eloquent missive proclaimed that the intimacy they'd shared—however brief and improper—was something she'd always treasure. She confessed her inexperience in such matters, said she understood that Camille—surely a veteran in the complexities of sapphic love—would find nothing too much of interest in an ingénue like herself, but that she simply couldn't bear to be married without ever having known even an ounce of true pleasure.

The very next Sunday, the profound effects of that letter became apparent. While the other girls were mooning at Frederick over the back fence, Maddie happened by Camille in the hall. She was fixing pins in her outing hat as the house's private horse-drawn carriage waited for her in the driveway, ready to whisk her off to the train station for her weekly disappearance.

"Ah, Maddie! There you are!" She beamed. "I'm engaged to meet some friends in London. Might you like to accompany me?"

A trip? Alone with Camille? The invitation required no contemplation. Maddie ran up the stairs, grabbed her own outing hat, and joined Camille in the carriage, not giving a single thought to where precisely they were headed. It didn't matter. For the first time since their latest indiscretion, things felt easy between them. There was no awkwardness. Camille was relaxed, jovial, and swiftly put Maddie out of her misery.

"You did nothing wrong," she said, slapping a tight lid on the matter. "The transgression was entirely mine. Let's not agonize over it."

And so they didn't. When they arrived in London, Camille steered them to a western part of the city that Maddie found entirely unfamiliar. Not that she considered herself anything more than a tourist in any quarter of the capital, but this one was particularly foreign to her.

The streets were filled with women of all varieties, and a good many of them seemed to recognize Camille. They wore brightly-colored feathers in their hats—if they wore hats at all—

and held their skirts a few inches too high as they walked.

"Wherever are we?" Maddie took Camille's crooked arm as it was offered to her.

"Leicester Square," Camille replied, keeping Maddie close. "I come here nearly every week. Isn't it delightful? So vibrant. So much to look at."

Maddie wasn't sure whether she referred to the elaborate garden at the center of the square or to the women who congregated in it, but readily agreed in either case. Later, she learnt that the whole place was known to be a veritable hive of iniquity, and she ought to have guessed as much when the establishment Camille brought her to was filled with scantily-clad women who sat much too freely on the laps of men.

Fortunately, they didn't linger near those rooms. Camille took her by the hand and led her up the back staircase, and the higher they rose on the crooked, uneven steps, the stronger the scent of perfume became. Not just one variety but several, all swirling together. The heady floral bouquet hinted at the presence of many women, and sure enough, when they emerged from the darkened passage, there was not a man in sight—much to Maddie's very great relief.

These upper rooms were three in number and decked out lavishly: silk wallpaper, velvet sofas, and imported rugs. Colored netting hung from the ceiling like a great canopy, filtering the light from the wall sconces and casting the space in shades of purples and pinks.

With every step into this decadent paradise, Camille was greeted like an old friend, receiving hugs and cheek kisses aplenty, and it seemed to

Maddie that all who came into contact with her fell under a sort of spell.

"These are your friends?" she questioned, her stomach twisting in a knot when one woman tendered Camille a kiss directly on the lips.

"Friends and acquaintances." Camille paid for two glasses of champagne at the bar and directed Maddie to an unoccupied sofa at the edge of the room.

"Is this a party?" Maddie accepted one of the glasses, keenly anticipating the relaxing effect a little booze was likely to have on Camille's temperament.

"Not exactly." Camille draped her arm over the back of the sofa, nursing her own glass in her lap. "Though one might say that it's a celebration of love."

Her curiosity piqued by that, Maddie watched two women settle into one of the other sofas. At first glance, one could mistake their closeness for a familial bond. Their knees touched. Their hands were interlocked. Their eyes never left each other. Then they kissed. Their ravenous lips met with passion, dispelling all doubt about the true nature of their love, and heat rose in Maddie's face. She could do nothing to hide it.

"You color up beautifully." Camille brushed the back of her hand over one of Maddie's reddened cheeks. "I hope you're not too uncomfortable?"

Maddie shook her head and sipped her champagne. "I'm glad to be with you. This is where you disappear to on Sundays?"

"In search of company, yes." Camille pressed an impulsive kiss on the side of her head. "I've never brought anyone here before, but I wanted you to see it."

"Why?" Maddie leant back, a shiver running through her when she felt Camille's arm close in around her shoulders.

"Because it's important for you to know that, no matter what your path in life may be, there are outlets for your passions. Do you understand? You will never be alone in your desire."

Maddie's heart sank. Was that the purpose of this outing? To encourage her to expand the horizons of her interests? She peered up at Camille, hoping she was wrong. "You wish for me to turn my attentions elsewhere?"

"I wish for you to be happy," Camille corrected her. "You seek experience in these pursuits—you are hungry for it—and to that end, you need not settle for me." She gestured to the room. "Look around. There's so much more."

"Settle for you?" Maddie shook her head, rejecting that. "I want no other woman. There's none in the world more beautiful than you in any case."

"Is that so?" Camille's eyebrow shot up. "And how much of the world have you seen?"

No answer.

"Darling, it's sweet of you to be so kind, but let's not pretend." She hooked a finger under Maddie's chin and turned her head. "I'm much too old for you. This is foolish."

Maddie didn't see the age in her. She was blind to it. There were certainly a few creases beside her eyes and lines where she smiled, but nothing that detracted from her beauty.

"It's all very well for you to say such things, but I shan't be dissuaded from you," she stated resolutely. "My heart is already set in the matter."

Those words took a few moments to sink in, then Camille recovered the ability to speak.

"Are you quite sure?" Her voice was whisper soft.

Maddie nodded. "I've read of it plenty. I know the feeling well."

"In that case, you're a very silly girl." Camille ran her thumb over Maddie's lips, her gaze fixed there. "We shall be the ruin of each other."

Before Maddie could prepare for it, Camille downed her champagne and crushed their mouths together. Her smooth lips—coated with the carmine-tinted beeswax she used to enhance their natural color—were firm but gentle, and Maddie melted into her ... but it didn't last long. As though startled by her own temerity, Camille drew back, searching Maddie's face for any sign that such an overture was unwelcome. There was none.

After polishing off the other glass of champagne, she re-engaged Maddie's lips with renewed confidence. Half-reclining, her shoulders pressed to the cushions, she pulled Maddie to her chest, allowing the teen's clumsy, overeager hands to wander freely about her body, from garter to breast.

From that moment on, time was lost to them. Afternoon drifted into evening. They drank a little, talked much, kissed often, and by the end of the night, Maddie was quite an expert in all forms of oral caress. When they finally left the bawdyhouse—as Camille reluctantly confessed it was—they were running late to catch the last train. Too late in fact.

"Well, there's nothing else for it." Camille stared down the empty platform and planted both hands on her hips. "We must spend the night in London."

Maddie's heart pounded. "Where?"

"I shall find us accommodations, but I have only a little money."

Maddie heard that as a warning, but didn't understand what it meant until she was standing in a hotel bedroom, eyeing the room's only bed.

MADDIE COULDN'T MOVE. WHILE CAMILLE SAT ON the sofa by the window, divesting herself of hat, jacket, and boots, she stood like a statue, gaping at the enormous four-poster bed that dominated the candlelit hotel room.

"I hadn't enough coin for separate accommodations." Camille addressed the stunned look in her eyes. "If it displeases you to sleep with me, I shall keep to the sofa."

Maddie glanced at the sofa's overstuffed velvet cushions, then back to the feather-stuffed mattress and the quilted counterpane. It was not fright that had her so dumbstruck, but that she couldn't believe her luck. Still, she reined in her desperate excitement on the off chance that she was presuming too much about Camille's intentions.

"I could not bear to think of you in discomfort when there's a whole half of the bed unused." She perched on the vanity chair and removed her boots, tackling the laces with such clumsy haste that she got them all knotted up. "Whatever shall we wear, though?"

"Our shemmies will do." Camille began to shed the layers.

Not wanting to be behindhand with her, Maddie wrenched off her uncooperative boots and followed suit, facing her reflection in the cheval mirror beside the washstand.

She'd never spent much time scrutinizing her own form, but she did so then. Wearing nothing more than her undergarments, she compared her curves to Camille's, still adjusting to the extra inches she'd only recently gained.

"There's no need to be bashful." Camille whisked off her under-bodice, baring that lavish satin corset in all its glory. "We each have the same parts."

"But your parts are so much nicer." Maddie toyed with the waistband of her drawers, contemplating their removal.

"Nonsense." Camille chuckled. "You're truly beautiful. Look." She swept in behind Maddie and laid her hands on the teen's hips. "These full hips, this slender waist." She slid her hands up to the narrowest part of Maddie's waist. "And here." She brought her hands under Maddie's breasts and cupped them. "See how full and firm they are? You have nothing whatever to be ashamed of." She dropped a kiss on Maddie's bare shoulder. "You're perfectly formed."

She kept her hands employed on Maddie's charms awhile, making the small ruby tips stiff and prominent, then turned her attentions southward. "Do you not wish to remove these?" She fingered the drawstring fastening at the back of Maddie's drawers.

Maddie sank against Camille's chest. "Ought I?" She lolled her head on Camille's shoulder. "We shall be so exposed to one another all night."

"You did not seem to mind being so exposed to me last week." Camille spun her around and held her by the waist. "Has your diffidence returned?"

"Perhaps a little." Maddie touched a finger to Camille's corset and traced invisible patterns in the satin, not daring to unfasten the stiff garment. "Will you have me tonight?"

Camille groaned, palpably pained to reject the offer. "Let's not get carried away with ourselves." She pecked Maddie's forehead, stepped away, and let down her waist-length hair. "I'm weakening to you, that is true, but these few little transgressions of ours must be enough." She paused, then repeated the sentiment with more conviction. "They *must*."

But they weren't. Openly disappointed, Maddie gazed at Camille's silky honey-colored mane and fought the urge to bury her face in it. Worsening her struggle for command over her basic impulses, she watched as Camille dropped her petticoat to the floor for the purpose of conducting her various nightly ablutions. Her diaphanous chemise exposed everything beneath, and Maddie gasped at the sight. She wore no drawers! Whatever would her mother think of a woman who crossed her legs at the knee *and* went about bare beneath her skirts?

"Oh, you've not got a stitch on you in the way of southern under things." She wasn't sure where to look.

"Does that concern you?" Camille retreated to the sofa and continued undressing. As she inched up her chemise to begin the business of rolling down her stockings, she revealed Maddie's red satin hair ribbon fastened around her thigh.

She blushed then, which was such a rarity that Maddie made note of it. Had she forgotten it was there? Why *was* it still there? Had she not the funds to replace her broken garter? Was she so impecunious? Maddie doubted that, and the thought was thoroughly dispelled when Camille unfastened the ribbon, unveiling a brand new garter elastic beneath.

"I'm a sentimental creature." Camille worked her stockings off. "I cannot help it."

Every time she moved, her breasts threatened to spill from her corset, and Maddie made the most of the unprecedented view. Not knowing when she might have such unreserved access to Camille's body again—if ever—she did her best to permanently imprint every glorious detail on her mind.

"They are not so firm as yours." Camille caught her staring. "Age is acting upon me I'm afraid." She unhooked the exquisite garment and released herself. "This is the body of a woman two decades your senior."

True enough, her unfettered breasts did not hold themselves as high as Maddie's—the difference was slight, but perceptible—but Maddie did not care. They were perfect.

"Here." Camille took her hand. "Feel." She laid Maddie's hand upon one of her weighty breasts. "What do you think?" She squeezed the orb into Maddie's palm.

Maddie whined. Perhaps they were not quite as youthful as they once were, but they were large and soft. Her proud, erect nipples demanded attention, and Maddie lowered her head to suck one into her mouth, wetting the fabric of Camille's chemise with her tongue.

"Oh, my sweet darling." Camille let her suckle for a minute before unlatching her. "Are you ready for bed?"

Truth be told, Maddie was anything but tired. She lingered by the bedside as Camille flung back the counterpane and slid onto the cool sheets, her thin cotton chemise bunching around her upper thighs, very nearly uncovering the triangular shadow of her pubic thatch.

"You wish to see it?" Camille volunteered her body for further exploration.

Without waiting for a response—not that Maddie was capable of one—she lay down and turned up the hem of her chemise, displaying the hallowed ground between her legs.

It was immaculate. Her blonde curls were trimmed short, scarcely concealing the pouty lips of her sex. Her pearl hid at the apex of her cleft, but as she raked her fingers through the small quantity of hair on her motte, she coaxed it out.

"Come to bed," she cooed. "Let me look at you as well. No-one ever came to any harm for looking."

Realizing she was still wearing an impractical amount of clothing, Maddie fumbled hastily with her knee-length drawers and kicked them off as soon as they fell to her ankles. She gave no thought to her stockings or her garters— but Camille did. As she clambered into bed and tugged up her shemmy, revealing the dark bloom between her thighs, Camille's eyes were pinned to her right garter.

"Is that mine?" She fingered the ruffled black lace and satin bow. "You fixed it."

Maddie covered it with her hand and opened her mouth to apologize, but never got a word out.

"I hoped you would." Camille bent to kiss it. "I'm glad you did." She trailed a fingertip beyond the garter, up Maddie's thigh and over her mossy outcrop, in full admiration of her form. "You are surely God's most divine creation."

For several minutes, they lay in worship of one another. Their lips met for more kisses, Maddie helped herself to Camille's chemise-covered breasts, and it seemed for a while that any reservations Camille had were cast to the wind. Then there was a halting.

"We ought to get some rest if we're to make the first train tomorrow." Camille disengaged herself from Maddie's groping hand. "It's gone midnight already, I'm sure."

Dissatisfied with the prospect of simply rolling over and going to sleep, Maddie remained in Camille's embrace, reluctant to move. "Is there nothing more we could do?"

Having read more than her fair share of bawdy sapphic literature, she knew there was plenty more they *could* do ... if only Camille would allow it.

"My darling, we've already done far too much." Camille pulled her chemise back into place. "Please try to understand my position."

Maddie didn't. She couldn't. It was utterly unfathomable to her. She was of age, and Camille was unmarried. What other obstacle was there?

"Blow out the candle," Camille prompted her. "I'm exhausted. It's been an eventful day."

Thoroughly huffed, Maddie flopped resignedly onto her back. "I shall if I must—if you must rob me of the sight of you as well as the touch—but I do not think I can sleep, and it's entirely your fault."

"Why?" Camille yawned. "Whatever's the matter?"

"I've not yet given myself a relief," Maddie grumbled. "My body's grown quite accustomed to the pleasure as it is, and your kisses have made it ever so hot tonight."

A silence crept in before Camille responded cautiously. "I shan't object if you feel the need."

Permission granted, Maddie wasted no time. She began the work immediately, only to pause in the midst of it when she heard a muted whimper from the other side of the bed and discovered Camille engaged in the same operation.

"Are you doing it as well?" She tugged back the covers for visual confirmation.

"Yes." Camille mewled, tickling her sex. "Forgive me."

No forgiveness was necessary.

"Let us do it together." Maddie rolled closer. "Please do!"

Camille had little choice in that; she had no path of retreat. Side by side, they indulged in their manipulations, their busy hands bumping against one another. It was torture.

Brave in that moment, Maddie's hand abandoned its post and breached the narrow gap between their heaving bodies. Receiving no objection but a pitiful whine, her tentatively encroaching fingertips met first with the tight curls on Camille's mound, then strove toward the furrow and dipped between her puffy labia, drawing moisture from the innermost well of her lust-drenched article up to her swollen, hardened pearl.

"Oh, my darling, yes!" Camille surrendered, clutched Maddie to her chest, and brought a reciprocal hand to her treasure. A minute later, they were quivering together, their voluptuous cries smothered with each other's mouths.

MADDIE WOKE IN CAMILLE'S ARMS AND SOUGHT A kiss—which Camille gave freely. She had no idea of the time. The heavy velvet curtains shielded the room from the glare of the gaslights in the street at night, and any sign of daybreak come morning, but she was certain they'd slept in past dawn. Regardless, Camille seemed to be in no hurry to rise. She lay with her hand on Maddie's bare rump, keeping their bodies held tight together, skin touching skin, their shemmies rucked up around their middles, and granted kisses upon request.

"You're far too irresistible, my love." She gave Maddie's bum a squeeze and sighed heavily. "I have succumbed."

"Is it so terribly bad?" Maddie couldn't believe that it was. "We had the greatest pleasure together, didn't we?"

"We most certainly did." Camille rolled them over and planted herself between Maddie's thighs, her tousled blonde hair tumbling over her

65

shoulders. "But now I'm afraid I want so much more."

Maddie had no idea what to expect. In fact, the first time Camille moved her hips, causing their pearls to rub together and a bolt of electricity to shoot through her core, she thought it accidental. Then it happened again. And again. The fourth time, it was accompanied by the faintest whimper from Camille's lips, and then she knew: they were entwined in the most sacred embrace.

"Oh, please!" She wrapped her legs around Camille's hips, assuming the position she'd read about in so many books. "I do so want you!"

As the friction began to have an undeniable effect, their flushed sexes weeping with their combined passion, something Camille once said during dance instruction struck her: Your movements must be sympathetic to mine. Feel the motion of my body.

With that in mind, she matched Camille's rhythm as best she could and met each thrust with a corresponding shove of her pelvis, so ensuring that their parts came fully together, their pearls kissing with every stroke.

"That's it!" Camille encouraged her. "You're a natural!" She clutched Maddie's rump hard, her manicured fingernails digging into the teen's flesh. "You must have your pleasure with me." Her exertions became strained as her crisis neared. "Spend! Spend! Spend!"

"It's happening." Maddie wailed, beginning to shudder. "Oh, you're doing it to me!"

Her bum jerked and twitched as Camille bore down on her, their lust-slickened articles

THE RUIN OF US

gliding together as they came, their bodies seized
with contractions.

THE TRAIN RIDE BACK TO THE HOUSE WAS FILLED with furtive glances, stolen kisses, and subtle touches. They hadn't washed since they rubbed each other into delirium in the hotel bed, and Maddie's drawers dampened with fresh excitement to know that the residue of Camille's amatory fluid was smeared all over her aching, impatient sex.

Her passions were far from sated, and she pawed on Camille at every opportunity. Upon their arrival at the house, she hoped to make one more desperate bid for intimacy before returning to the mundanity and formality of everyday life, but her plans were thwarted by the presence of a curvaceous brunette who saw their carriage draw up and met them in the entrance hall.

"Ah, there you are at last! I was getting worried." The woman greeted Camille with outstretched arms. "Wherever have you been?"

Camille dropped Maddie's hand like a hot coal and welcomed the brunette into a hug. "I'm afraid we did such a silly thing and missed the last train yesterday." She accepted a peck on the lips. "We had to remain in London for the night."

"How frightfully dull for you." The woman laughed. "I hope this little chit was good company at least." She waved a dismissive hand in Maddie's direction.

At being called a chit—an immature young girl—Maddie clenched her jaw. She may have been a mere girl when she left the house yesterday afternoon, but thanks to Camille, she had most certainly returned a woman.

"Off you go now and clean yourself up." The brunette proceeded to shoo her away like she were some bothersome pest. "You'll be needing a wash, I expect."

Before complying, Maddie flashed Camille a look. Why was this stranger issuing such orders? And why ought she follow them? She wanted answers, but Camille neither explained nor belayed the command. She merely put on a weak smile, nodded, and confirmed the instruction, giving Maddie no choice but to obey it.

"Enjoy the rest of the day. Lessons will resume in the morning."

Defeated, Maddie slunk upstairs, but she had no intention of washing. En route to her bedroom, her mind reeling with questions, she discovered a group of the older girls gossiping together in one of the other rooms and stopped by the open door to listen.

"How long is she back for this time?" one asked. "I do hope it goes by quickly. Miss Camille is always so vexed by her presence."

Needing answers, Maddie butted in. "Who is she? Who is the woman downstairs?"

"We are to call her Miss Hannah," the girl replied. "Camille's friend."

"Ha! What do you know of it?" Sarah, the eldest of the bunch, laughed. "They are far more to each other than that."

Maddie clung to the doorframe. "Whatever do you mean?"

"Once, when I had a dreadful sickness, I rose from my bed to ask if I might be given a drop of medicine to help me sleep. It was past midnight, but Miss Camille was not to be found in her room—she was in Miss Hannah's. And the noises coming from within! Lor'!"

"What noises?" Maddie scarcely dared to ask.

"The absolute naughtiest kind." Sarah giggled, then performed a perfect rendition of the soft whimpers and whines Maddie had relished hearing from Camille's lips that very morning.

"Were they flat-cocking?" the first girl asked with a frown.

"I daresay." Sarah shrugged. "I peeped through the keyhole and saw Miss Hannah on her back like this." She flung herself onto the bed, crooked her knees to the ceiling, and wiggled her fleshy bum.

"I've heard of such a thing, but fail to see what pleasure it can bring without the proper organ." The frowning girl looked thoroughly perplexed. "How is it done?"

"Quite like this!" Another girl dived on top of Sarah and played the part of Camille, rutting on her and humping the air between her legs.

"Oh, Camille!" Sarah immediately assumed the role of Hannah and writhed beneath her. "Rub our things together! Do!"

Maddie felt sick. The girls kept their performance going until hearty laughter erupted, then Sarah flung a pillow in Maddie's direction.

"I bet Maddie knows all about flat-cocking anyway." She smirked. "You do, don't you, Maddie? Isn't that what you were doing with Miss Camille all night in London?"

That was too much. Tears pricking her eyes, Maddie ran to her room, slammed the door, and fell upon the bed, smothering her sobs in the counterpane.

WITHIN DAYS, ALL PLEASANTNESS CAME UNDONE. As the other girls predicted, there was a change in Camille when Hannah was about, as if her mere presence stifled Camille's spirit. The house fell quiet, void of laughter. Lessons took on a more serious tone. A heavy air of gloom hung over everything Camille said and did, and there were no more trips to the lake. Worse still, she grew distant.

There was no prolonged eye contact, no shared smiles, and absolutely no precious touches—nor anything that could be construed as such. When Maddie reached for her hand, she withdrew. Was the measure of her devotion being tested? Or her patience?

Unable to sleep one night, Maddie rose and snuck down to the library. She intended to pick out a book and read until her sight blurred and consciousness petered out, but on her way back to bed, a light in the parlor stopped her. Book in hand, she changed course and found Camille reading by candlelight in her armchair beside the fireplace.

"May I join you?"

Camille hesitated before she looked up. "Of course." She dropped a hand toward Maddie's usual spot beside her. "Please."

They hadn't been alone since London—Camille had made sure of that—and Maddie's heart pounded as she crossed the room to sit at her feet. She felt like she was breaking some unwritten law, and violated it further when, several minutes later, she dared to speak.

"Does Miss Hannah displease you?" She knew she had no business questioning their private affairs, but did so anyway.

"Whatever makes you ask such a thing?"

"There's a sadness in you when she's around. A coldness, too." Maddie lost all desire to read. "You aren't the same with me, and I fear that you're casting me adrift."

"It's a complicated business." Camille laid a hand on Maddie's shoulder. "Please don't let it trouble you, or think that I've grown dull on you." The hand stayed. "I am restrained with you only because I must be, and you must be patient. All will resume in due course."

All? What was 'all'? The occasional illicit rub in a London hotel? Chaste admiration from a distance? Stolen kisses in the house's private carriage? Maddie was confused. Until the sudden appearance of Hannah, she thought they were embarking upon a romance. A dangerous romance with high stakes and much secrecy, but a romance nonetheless. In reality, she feared, it wasn't anything more than a fleeting amour: a sordid affair.

While continuing to read, Camille's hand wandered. She ran her fingers under Maddie's hair and tickled the nape of her neck, unwittingly stirring the teen into a passion.

"Oh, I cannot bear it!" Maddie tossed her book aside and swept her hands under Camille's skirts, throwing them up and crumpling them in her lap. "I love you, I love you, I love you!" She brought her lips to Camille's ankle, shin, knee, and above.

"Stop," Camille pled weakly, her heavy book tumbling from her grasp and hitting the floor with a clattering thud.

"I don't want to." Maddie kept kissing, professing her love at every interval until she reached the top of Camille's stockings. There, she faltered.

The red ribbon around Camille's garter was gone.

"I'm sorry." Camille saw her distress. "It has to be this way."

Maddie wasn't interested in hearing that. Her fervor dampened—but not entirely extinguished—by the disappointing discovery, she lowered her face into Camille's lap and burrowed her nose between the older woman's tightly-crossed thighs, drowning herself in the scent of her peachy skin and the natural perfume of her femininity.

"Let me kiss it just this once." She pushed Camille's skirts up higher, baring the blanket of blonde curls ornamenting her mound, her pearl— and everything below it—infuriatingly hidden from view. "Let me see how it weeps."

She drove forward, targeting that moss with her lips, and the tension in Camille's thighs dissipated. Her limbs loosened, allowing them to be pried apart, and she eased her hips forward, spreading her legs around Maddie's shoulders.

"Oh, dear God, forgive me." She buried her fingers in Maddie's hair and coaxed her toward the pink furrow. "Put your mouth to me, my love. I need it."

As Maddie's tongue found the seat of her pleasure and engulfed it, she bit her lower lip and smothered a moan. Lost to passion, she hooked one leg over Maddie's shoulder and raised her hips, straining to give the enthusiastic teen full access to her womanhood. In doing so, her head lolled against the chair back, facing the door.

The *open* door.

Where the maid was standing.

Thoroughly mortified, Camille shrieked and wrenched Maddie's head away from her loins. "Enough!" She lashed out and struck Maddie across the cheek with her open palm, the hit knocking her to the fireplace rug like a paper doll.

"Begging your pardon, Miss, but I came in when I heard a noise." The maid dipped her head. "Miss Hannah is asking for you."

Camille straightened her skirts and rose, wiping tears from her eyes. "I must go to her."

"Don't!" Maddie lunged for her ankles, clutching a fistful of her skirts.

"I *must*." Camille brushed her hands away and strode from the room, leaving her in a sobbing heap upon the floor.

Camille took a moment to gather herself before entering Hannah's bedroom. She didn't want to look as though she'd been upset, so she dabbed away the residual moisture clinging to her eyelashes and fixed her blotchy eye paint, hoping that would suffice.

Inside, Hannah awaited her on the bed. She was naked beneath a chiffon peignoir, her ruddy-brown hair let loose, and she smelt like lavender and chamomile. She'd just had a bath.

"Tend to me." She opened the peignoir. "My body hungers for your touch."

She was a beautiful woman. No-one could deny that. A life free from hardship and childbirth had allowed her to retain a fashionable figure, despite exceeding forty years of age. The color of her hair was aided by henna, obscuring the encroaching gray, and the lines on her face were easily concealed with a little powder. Tending to her physical needs was certainly no hardship, but Camille remained less than amenable to the prospect.

"Must we tonight?" She lingered by the vanity. "I'm not feeling at my best."

"Are you ill?" Hannah sat up, showing concern for her only in as much as a cat is concerned for its human slave when dinner fails to arrive on time. "Come here." She patted the counterpane. "Let me look at you."

Camille obeyed, sitting meekly as Hannah felt her reddened cheeks and her temple, seeking evidence of a fever.

"You're so flushed." Hannah unbuttoned her clothing, finding that the heat had spread to her upper chest. "But perhaps it's not an illness that plagues you." She thrust a hand up Camille's skirts and plunged two fingers between her plump labia, directly into her lubricious slit.

Camille yowled.

"It appears I've found the source of the problem." Hannah rubbed her thumb over Camille's swollen clit, her probing fingers working harder and deeper. "Whatever have you been doing?"

"Nothing." Camille whined pitifully, but made no attempt to stop her. "If I am in a state of passion, then it is only anticipation for you that has me so."

"Liar!" Hannah withdrew from her. "Which one is it? The new girl? That dear little foundling you took to London." She shoved Camille onto her back and straddled her. "Are you fucking her?"

Camille shook her head, but the fib was met with a sharp slap.

"How dare you!" Hannah slapped her again. "When I am away from this house, you may do as you please—you may have your little amusements, for no woman should be made to live without affection—but do not forget that it is me who allows you your dalliances at the house in London. It is *my* credit upon which you rely."

"What have they said to you?" Camille held her stinging cheek.

"Only that you brought another woman to the place. She was a very much younger woman, by all accounts—certainly no harlot—and you spent the better part of the evening with your wicked tongue in her mouth."

"This is the reason for your sudden return?" Camille speculated.

"You need to be reined in." Hannah pinned Camille's wrists above her head. "Are the whores I pay for not good enough for you anymore? You've become so lewd and desperate that you must bed a child of this house?"

"They're not children." Camille had the audacity to defend herself. "They're young women, and Maddie is not inclined toward the love of a man."

Another slap came. "You will not cavort with that little temptress anymore. Do you understand? You'll not touch her again. Ever. It's an embarrassment."

"What do you truly care?" Fresh tears welled in Camille's eyes. "You're too busy spending your father's money to give any thought for what goes on in this house."

"This house has *my* name above the door," Hannah snarled. "If you bring disgrace upon it, you bring disgrace upon my family." One more slap. "From now on, you *will* behave."

CAMILLE SAT IN A CHAIR BESIDE THE WINDOW, nursing an empty glass of brandy and fidgeting with a length of red satin ribbon fastened around her wrist: Maddie's hair ribbon. Behind her, Hannah slept soundly in the bed, sprawled nude under the covers, worn out from their couplings.

When seized in the grip of a wild passion, Hannah always became particularly demanding. She wanted pleasure in every conceivable attitude, and Camille was sore, her sex throbbing.

It was often Hannah's letch to possess her as a man would. For the purpose, she had a rigid rubber contrivance with leather straps which she tied around her hips and thighs, securing the makeshift priapic appendage to her core. With it in place, she could do much of a man's work, thrusting up and into Camille, rutting on her with unrelenting force, the tip of the hard phallus battering the gateway to her womb. All the while, she'd remind Camille of her place.

"You belong to me."

"This cunt is mine."

Miserable, and having depleted the supply of brandy kept in a decanter on the vanity, Camille got dressed and stole downstairs to her study. There was more booze locked in her sideboard. Lots more booze.

Well past bedtime, Maddie jolted awake on the parlor floor, startled into consciousness by the sound of smashing glass. After being rejected by Camille, she hadn't mustered the energy to move and so cried herself to sleep on the rug, remaining there long after Camille's reading candle guttered and died. There was still a wet spot made by her tears.

Groggy and disoriented, she got up, rubbed her puffy, crusty eyes, and listened for more noise, hearing only Camille's faint voice slurring a coarse oath. What was she doing up? Ought she not be in bed with Hannah? Curious, Maddie padded to Camille's study and peeked in, finding her slumped on the floor, picking clumsily at the remains of a shattered brandy glass, her unsteady hands visibly trembling.

"Leave it." Maddie pushed open the door and entered. "You'll cause yourself an injury."

Bleary-eyed, Camille squinted in her direction. "You shouldn't be in here." She backhanded moisture from her clammy cheeks, her rouge streaked and smudged. "It's late."

"I wanted to make sure you were all right." Maddie knelt beside her. "I upset you earlier." She clasped her hands together in her lap and kept her head down. "I was disobedient."

"My sweet darling, you did nothing wrong and I ... I struck you." Camille winced. "I'm so sorry." She reached a hand to Maddie's cheek, cupped it, and leant forward to kiss the chastised skin. "I don't want to hurt you any more than I already have, but I will if we keep on."

"Whatever do you mean?" Maddie nuzzled Camille's palm, glad of any physical contact.

"It's all well and good when the amusement is simply that, but when it isn't ... when the dalliance becomes more ..." Camille shook her head and withdrew. "She cannot abide that."

"I don't understand." A frown creased Maddie's brow.

"It's of no importance." Camille returned to work on the glass.

"Enough!" Maddie scooped up her hands, forcing her to stop picking at the shards for fear that she might prick herself. "How much have you had to drink? You're in such a dreadful state."

As she pulled Camille's hands into her lap, she caught sight of the red satin ribbon wrapped around her wrist, otherwise concealed by the cuff of her dress. She recognized it immediately. Her hair ribbon!

"You haven't forsaken me!" She kissed it.

"Never." Camille slid a hand around Maddie's neck and brought their foreheads together. "But you know Hannah has forbidden it." She inched forward, maneuvering Maddie onto her back. "I cannot have you."

"She knows?" Maddie's chest tightened with panic.

"She always knows." Camille eased Maddie's knees apart and crawled between them. "I am not permitted to love, or to *be* loved."

"What is it that binds you to her?" Maddie mewled as Camille tore down her drawers.

"Let's not speak of it tonight." Camille crushed their skirts between their bellies and fell forward, preparing to align their parts, but as she put out a hand to support her weight, a sliver of broken glass embedded itself in her palm.

She yelped and recoiled.

"Oh, no!" Maddie sat up and seized her bleeding extremity. "Hold still." She teased the jagged shard from Camille's ivory skin and bound the cut with a handkerchief from her pocket. "Let me take you to bed." She wriggled back into her drawers and heaved Camille up. "This mess will wait until morning."

She hooked Camille's arm around her shoulders and helped her up the stairs slowly and quietly, only to come face to face with Hannah at the top. She was standing in the hall outside Camille's bedroom, holding a candle, her entire body silhouetted behind the sheerest, most immodest peignoir Maddie had ever seen.

"Whatever's going on here?" the brunette demanded coldly.

"Miss Camille is not at her best." Maddie kept her propped up. "She had a little accident in her study, and I was bringing her to bed."

Hannah's eyes narrowed. "Very well." She stepped away from the door. "Bring her this way." She diverted Maddie from Camille's bedroom into her own.

84

Disinclined to dawdle, Maddie laid Camille upon the ruffled, sex-stained sheets of the four-poster and made for the door, but Hannah didn't let her get far.

"You like Miss Camille, yes?" She followed Maddie a little way into the hall so that they wouldn't be overheard. "And Miss Camille likes you, I can tell." She pursed her lips, scrutinizing Maddie's appearance. "That's a problem."

Maddie remained silent.

"She's been kind to you no doubt." Hannah took a slow walk around Maddie, picking at her dress and looking her up and down, making mental comparisons. "She's encouraged your affections and made you feel quite special—she's good at that."

"I'm not sure I know what you mean." Maddie played dumb.

"Nonsense," Hannah scoffed. "You girls obsess over her—you can't help it—but these foolish adolescent fancies pass quickly, and Camille knows better than to jeopardize herself." She eyed Maddie contemptuously. "She may have lost her way with you in London, but I can assure you she will not make that mistake again, and you must not allow yourself to love her."

"The heart is its own master," Maddie mumbled. "It cannot be told what to feel."

"Think as you please, but I say these things for your own good." Hannah sent her on her way. "Loving her would not be in your best interests." She turned toward her own room. "Besides, you wouldn't want her if you knew what she truly was." She slammed the door, leaving Maddie alone to contemplate the meaning of those words.

In fact, Maddie did a lot of contemplating that night. First, she contemplated what secrets Camille could possibly be harboring about herself that would make her undesirable, but she couldn't think of anything. She even drew up a list.

If Camille had deserted a husband somewhere, she would understand. If Camille had committed some crime—perhaps killing such a husband—she was certain it would be forgivable. If Camille had an extra toe, she would overlook it. If Camille were utterly penniless, she wouldn't care. If Camille had previously been a frog, enchanted into human form by a kiss, she would not mind in the least. Not even if she were a toad.

When that topic of thought was exhausted, each possibility becoming more ludicrous than the last, she tiptoed into the hallway and contemplated the sinful noises emanating from Hannah's bedroom. They started off faint and sporadic, but steadily increased in frequency and intensity until Maddie felt her eardrums might burst. Yet she couldn't walk away. She had to know: Were they Camille's desperate cries of passion? Or Hannah's?

In search of answers, she crept down the hall and peered through the keyhole, her stomach twisting in a knot to find Camille and Hannah nude on the bed. Camille's face was buried between Hannah's spread thighs, and as Hannah appeared to near the pinnacle of her pleasure, her mouth got away with her.

"Oh, you lewd bitch." She clutched a fistful of Camille's hair. "You're such a wicked whore."

Shocked to hear such foul language—directed at dearest, sweetest Camille, no less!—Maddie stumbled away from the keyhole and ran back to her room, the floorboards creaking beneath her feet.

MADDIE ROSE AT DAWN, HAVING SLEPT NOT A wink, and cleared up the broken glass in Camille's study before sitting alone in the breakfast room, waiting for the rest of the house to wake. What she had seen ate at her heart. She felt miserable, but perhaps not quite as miserable as Camille.

When Camille arrived in the breakfast room—her wounded hand freshly bandaged by the matron—she was clearly bearing the ill-effects of her overindulgence. She sat at her usual table with her head in her hands, drank only water, barely ate, and left as soon as Hannah relieved her to do so. She spoke to no-one else and never once broke a smile.

Since it was a Sunday, there was little to be done after the usual Godly obligatories. Assuming Hannah had plans to dominate much of Camille's free time, and not daring to make a bid for her attentions in any case, Maddie kept out of the way as best she could. Once the midday heat waned to a more comfortable level, she took a book and a blanket and went to Camille's spot beneath the tree at the lakeside. There, she read passages in fits and starts, her concentration broken by gazing intermittently at the lake.

"Thinking of going in?" Camille startled her, and she lost her page.

"Oh, damn and bugger." She leafed through the book, not at all sure where she was or why it mattered. She hadn't been enjoying herself.

"If you want to swim, I'll watch." Camille sounded painfully hopeful. "Like always."

Sadly, watching was no longer good enough. Maddie shook her head.

"May I join you, then?" Camille pressed on.

She had a book held to her chest, but Maddie guessed it to be little more than a ruse to get out of the house without being subjected to an interrogation.

"Where's Miss Hannah?" Maddie glanced around, as if the cruel brunette might be lurking in some shrubbery like a spy ready for ambush.

"Out." Camille tossed her book onto the grass and sat close.

One hand immediately strayed to Maddie's waist, but came to an abrupt halt when Maddie involuntarily flinched.

"Whatever's wrong?" She shrank back. "Have you grown dull on me? I wouldn't blame you. I must've been a frightful sight last night. You caught me drowning my sorrows."

"What sorrows?" Maddie picked idly at a disheveled page corner.

"Nothing as could be so easily explained in a few simple words." Camille sat sideways, heels to bum, her shoulder propped against the tree

90

trunk. "But if I did anything whatever to upset you, then I am deeply sorry."

"It was not what you did then that upset me." Maddie closed up her book and abandoned it. "It was what I witnessed after, in Miss Hannah's room."

"I was afraid that was you." Camille cringed. "I heard footsteps."

"You were giving her pleasure." Maddie slipped into a sulk.

"Oh, my love." Camille shuffled closer. "I did only what I had to do."

"What you *had* to do?" Maddie glared at her. "Who *has* to do such things? What hold does Miss Hannah have over you?" She demanded answers. "Who is this woman?"

Camille shrugged. "When I met her, she was a spinster heiress who'd brought much shame and aggravation upon her parents by refusing to marry. To separate himself from his parental failure, her father gave her an annuity and set her up in this house, intending to keep her busy and away from society life, but she never wanted it." Camille glanced back at the house, visible in the distance beyond the sprawling gardens and scattered apple trees. "It's her house in name only. She has no interest in the running of it and comes and goes as she pleases, like a feral cat."

"You do not love her."

"I've tried to." Camille sighed. "I wish I could." She lolled her head against the tree. "Oh, how much easier my life would be if I did."

"What is it, then?" Maddie tucked her knees up and fit herself into the space between Camille's crooked legs and the tree, effectively sitting in her lap. "What is it that has you bound so severely that you would deny yourself happiness? Can you not tell me?" She reached up and laid her palm against Camille's face. "Why give yourself to a woman who calls you a bitch and a whore? The vilest of all names."

"I *am* a whore." Camille shocked her. "Since I was fifteen years old."

Maddie drew back slightly. "That cannot be true."

"But it is." Camille swept an arm around her waist, anchoring her, preventing any further retreat. "My mother was the same way before she caught a pox, sold me, and did away with herself, so I suppose one might say that it's a family business."

"Your mother sold you?" Maddie made no effort to hide her distaste.

"To the first man who wanted me." Camille grimaced at the mention of him. "He took me to London as his mistress, but I fled from him and soon fell into a bad life." She swallowed hard. "A regrettably immoral life, from which I found it impossible to escape."

"And Hannah?" Maddie wondered where she appeared in the equation.

"I was not much past twenty when Hannah first came to me," Camille recalled. "By that time, I was working at a bawdyhouse in the vicinity of Leicester Square."

"The place you brought me to," Maddie supposed. "You're well-known there."

Camille nodded, shaking a single tear loose. "Hannah visited often and took a firm liking to me. I was a popular commodity in those days: young, clean, and beautiful. In time, she made an offer to pay my debts—of which I had many—and took me away from the place, promising to keep me as her wife."

"Her pet," Maddie sneered.

"Either way, she bought me." Camille didn't debate the various possible definitions of her captivity. "It's been over a decade now, and I've grown moderately content with my lot, though she never lets me forget my less than respectable provenance."

"She cages you."

"She *owns* me," Camille insisted. "I had nothing before I met her, and I have nothing now. Only what she gives to me. Every stitch of every silk dress belongs to her."

That quieted Maddie for a while, then, "She told me not to love you."

"She's right." Camille was neither surprised nor outraged. "I'm not worthy of you. You're too good for the likes of me."

"Never say that." Maddie shook her head vehemently. "I'm the *same* as you: a girl fished from the gutter and thrown into a better life."

"Do I not disgust you?"

"Not one damn bit." Maddie threw herself at Camille's chest, capturing her in an embrace. "I've been told that my real mother was as you were. That is to say, she found money in company. She had no other choice."

"Many don't."

"Before she died, she gave me up so that I might have the opportunity to improve myself, but I cannot be the daughter these people want me to be." Maddie pulled a folded up letter from her pocket. "See here." She thrust it at Camille. "The father of this boy they intend for me to marry is sending a doctor here tomorrow. He is to verify that I am untouched, and if I am proven to be impure, they will not want me. They shall call the wedding off."

"Well, you needn't fret about that." Camille sent the letter the way of her book. "I've done nothing to compromise you in that way."

"You misunderstand me." Maddie tried to articulate herself better. "I've read of a contrivance that mimics the work of a man's article. Do you know of such a thing?"

Camille nodded. "Rather intimately as it so happens. Why?"

"Do you possess one?" Maddie's eyes lit up. "Please say that you do."

"Yes, but—"

"Use it upon me," Maddie begged. "Do what must be done."

Camille whined in disbelief. "You wish for me to ruin you?"

"I wish for you to free me," Maddie clarified the request. "Don't you see?"

"Free you?" Camille massaged her furrowed brow and groaned. "My darling, if you shame yourself, your parents will abandon you."

"They might, but I don't damn well care." Maddie wouldn't hear a word against the scheme and remained glued to the proposition. "Come to my room tonight. Do!"

"How can I?" Camille held her close. "Hannah would surely find out."

"There is no choice in the matter." Maddie clung to her bodice. "If it is to be done—if I'm to be spared a life of possession by a man—it must be done tonight."

CAMILLE GOT DRESSED AND PERCHED ON THE EDGE of the bed, watching Hannah sleep. How had things turned so sour between them? She didn't know. Her feelings for Hannah changed on a daily basis. Some days, she was consumed with pure hatred. Others, it was pity. Mostly, it was regret.

They had fun in the beginning, though. Camille, being grateful for the change in circumstance, sought to please her in every way, and she was a delight to be near. When did she grow so cold? So cruel? She wasn't always that way. It came with the years, each one more dismal than the last. She became bitter and resentful, and their intimacy became a battle of wills. She wanted more of Camille than Camille could give. She wanted love.

Gradually, as she came to accept defeat in the matter, her trips grew longer and more frequent. She returned to the house only to sate her physical needs and to remind Camille of her place. It seemed purely out of spite that she refused to set her free.

"Forgive me," Camille whispered, and leant over the bed to kiss her forehead.

It was time. She'd kept Maddie waiting long enough.

Maddie awoke with a sense of someone else being in the room. What was the hour? She hadn't meant to fall asleep. Expecting Camille's arrival imminently, she'd cast the room in candlelight, stripped to her chemise, and tested out a variety of seductive poses upon the bed. Evidently, the last pose had proven far too comfortable.

In front of her, positioned on the bedside table so that she would see it all when she opened her eyes, was a bottle of brandy and two glasses. Beside them lay a long phallic object attached to two leather straps.

"Oh, lummy ..." She sat up to get a better look and felt heat move in behind her.

"Do you still want this, my darling?" Camille held her by the waist and nuzzled her neck. "If you have any doubts, tell me now."

Maddie shook her head. "It's the only way."

She reached for the rubber phallus and held it in her palm, awed by its thickness. When she wrapped her fingers around the shaft of the thing, her thumb and forefinger did not quite meet, and the bulbous head looked truly monstrous.

Glancing again at the bedside table, she saw that the brandy bottle was open and one glass had been recently used. There was a smear of Camille's tinted lip paste on the rim.

"What purpose the brandy?"

"Courage." Camille buried her face in Maddie's hair. "I've never done this before," she confessed in a whisper. "Brought a girl fully into womanhood, that is."

"I should hope not." Maddie giggled. "I would not like to think that you make a habit of it." She inspected the hefty priapus more closely, estimating it to be a full seven inches from root to tip. "Will it hurt?"

"It might." Camille sounded apologetic.

"How is it to be done?" Maddie pondered the slight curve in its shape, the concave base, and the straps attached to it. "Ought I prepare myself in any way? I've heard that the titillation of fingers may be used to relax the channel and ease its introduction. Is that true? I thought perhaps we could begin with that, then—"

"Sshhh." Camille hushed her. "Don't fuss. I don't want it to be like that."

"Like what?" Maddie frowned.

"Medical. Sterile. Unfeeling." Camille sighed and flopped onto her back. "If I am to do this, I shan't do it because it *must* be done, I shall only do it because ..." She hesitated.

"Because why?" Maddie wanted to hear her say it.

"Because I want to. Because I love you."

Maddie heard a smile in Camille's voice and spun around to gush her own undying love in return, but all the words got stuck in her throat. Camille was naked. The pale orbs ornamenting her chest were proudly on display, her nipples stiff, as if straining to be touched, and Maddie couldn't look anywhere else. They had a mesmerizing effect.

"Does this body please you?" Camille awaited appraisal.

"This body is perfect." Maddie wetted the tip of her forefinger and circled one of Camille's nipples, causing it to swell more. "How much time do we have?" She scooped the whole breast into her palm, watching goose bumps prick the surrounding flesh.

"Plenty." Camille murmured. "I did an unconscionably naughty thing, and am certain I shall be sent straight to hell for it." She smirked wickedly. "I slipped a sleeping draught into Hannah's bedtime drink. She will not wake."

Assured that there was no reason to hurry, Maddie's exploratory fingers continued their timid ministrations a while longer. "If we are not to be rushed, will you do to me what I saw you do to her? You were using your mouth upon her as I used mine upon you, and I should like to know the pleasure it brings."

Emboldened by Camille's unabashed nudity, she took a deep breath and whisked off her chemise. Naked but for Camille's garter around her thigh, she presented herself for touching, and Camille responded with gusto.

In an instant, the covers were flung away and Camille's lips were all over her, kissing every inch from neck to breasts to belly ... and lower. Delightfully lower.

"Lie down, my darling." Camille laid her supine, limbs spread. "Let me taste you."

A moment later, she brought her eager, hungry mouth to Maddie's sex, moaning into her drenched flesh.

The sensations were overwhelming. Maddie expected to feel the sweet caress of Camille's tongue on her southern parts, but not the accompaniment of fingers. As Camille kissed her pearl, two probing digits eased their way through her obstructed slit and she yowled. It was almost too much, but Camille applied such tender pressures that her crisis came with little resistance. In fact, it came too soon and was over too fast, leaving her in a fervor.

"You've made it hot." She writhed on the bed. "Do it to me now."

"If you're ready, my love." Camille backed off the bed and fastened the priapus around her waist and thighs so that it projected from her groin.

It was a perfect replica of the male member, just as Maddie had imagined.

"Are you quite certain of yourself?" Camille slathered the rigid piercer in cold cream and knelt in position between Maddie's legs. "There will be no denying what has occurred."

"I want you to have all of me." Maddie closed her eyes and braced herself. "Please."

Camille responded to her wish, and she felt the penetrating head of the priapus pushing at her opening. There was a slight stretching, a faint twinge of discomfort, then Camille gave a frightful shove. A sharp sting of pain shot through her core as her maidenhead gave way to the intrusion, and she suppressed a wail.

"There." Camille slid up her. "It has been done." She hilted herself. "How does it feel?"

Maddie made no sound.

"Darling, does it cause you pain? Do you not like it?" Camille kissed a tear away from the corner of her eye. "Do you wish for me to stop? Say the word and I—"

"No." Maddie gripped her buttocks, preventing her withdrawal. "Keep in." She slid both hands up Camille's back and pulled her into an embrace, their bodies locked tightly together. "Make me come."

THROUGHOUT THE NIGHT, MADDIE HAD HER pleasure thrice more. After each exquisite orgasm, Camille declared that she must return to Hannah's room, lest her absence be discovered, but she never once made any effort to decamp. The candles guttered and died, yet she remained entwined with Maddie until sunlight started to bleed through the curtains.

"I have to go." She sighed, disentangling herself from Maddie's clinging limbs. "Hannah will soon wake."

"So what if she does?" Maddie challenged her to make a stand. "Do you truly love me?"

"More than you'll ever know."

"Then leave this place." She swung a leg over Camille's lap, straddled her, and pushed her shoulders down, keeping her in the bed. "Run away with me."

"And go where?" Camille tucked Maddie's unkempt mop of dark hair behind her ears, preventing it from falling forward and obscuring her face. "I have nothing to offer you. What would we do for money? A return to my former employment would not be practical. I've not many good years left in me, and—"

"I wouldn't want that." Maddie cut her off. "Not ever."

"What, then?" Camille brought Maddie to her bosom with a sharp tug, seized her by the waist, and flipped them both over. "Tell me. What would you have me do without her?"

Tap, tap, tap.

The knocking on the door was barely perceptible, then it swung open.

"Young miss, there's a doctor here to see you. Shall I ..." The maid's voice trailed off. She stood in the doorway, gawping at the bed, soaking up the visual information.

Camille and Maddie were naked, hair in disarray. Camille's clothes were heaped at the foot of the bed. There was a dildo on the floor, abandoned on the rug, the light staining of defloration visible on the shaft. On the bedside table, there was the brandy—two glasses with it.

"What is it that you wish me to do?" She bowed her head as she spoke to Camille.

"Make him comfortable in the parlor." Camille's cheeks burned. "I shall be down directly."

As soon as the maid departed, she leapt out of bed and hurried into her clothes.

"Will she tell Hannah?" Maddie wasn't sure that would be a bad thing.

"I don't know, but we have more pressing concerns at the minute." Camille hid the phallus and all evidence of the brandy in the bedside table cupboard. "You must bear this indignity

102

first." She found Maddie's chemise dangling from the foot of the bed and urged her into it. "Wash yourself, then I will bring him to you." She turned to leave, but Maddie grabbed her hand.

"Kiss me." She pulled Camille back to the bedside. "Tell me you love me."

Camille softened, smiled, and sank onto the edge of the bed. "I love you." She kissed Maddie deeply. "Everything will be all right."

That was wishful thinking, but Maddie liked hearing it anyway.

Five minutes later, Camille—her blonde mane hastily introduced to a brush and swept into an up-do—knocked on her door as if she were a stranger to the room and led in a short white-haired man with a leather medical case.

"Present yourself," she instructed Maddie, affecting an austere tone. "This good doctor needs to inspect you." She hesitated then and addressed the white-haired man. "Ought I leave?"

From the bed, Maddie shook her head furiously.

"If the child wishes you to stay, you may stay." The doctor set his bag on the bedside table, next to an open jar of cold cream. "Now, my dear"—he patted Maddie on the head, as one would a dog—"this won't take long."

Before he could begin, the maid returned, unable to look Camille in the eye as she spoke.

"Miss Hannah's not yet arisen, and there's a telegram for her."

"Then wake her." Camille made no attempt to disguise the annoyance in her voice. "What do you bother me for?" She shooed the maid out and ushered the doctor on. "Hurry and do what you must."

"Covers down, knees up." The doctor donned a pair of wire-rimmed spectacles. "Quick as you please now."

As Maddie obeyed, a telltale pink wetness caught his eye on the sheets. He halted, glanced first at it, then at Maddie, then at Camille.

"What has been done here?" He gave a cursory glance up Maddie's chemise, reaching an instant and damning conclusion. "This girl has been breached."

Camille shrugged. "I am not a prison guard. I cannot keep these girls in at all times. They are adolescents; they will do what they will." She clasped her hands together so as not to fidget. "There's a local boy who delivers here once a week. Many of the girls have taken a fancy to him, and I presume it is he who is to blame."

The doctor caught a small smile on Maddie's lips. "Do you not even have the modesty left to feign any shame?"

He was about to turn his moral judgment upon Camille again, but was interrupted by the return of the maid. She burst in, breathing hard and in full panic.

"It's Miss Hannah." She pressed a hand to her chest. "I cannot wake her!"

Those words changed everything. In short order, the doctor pronounced Miss Hannah quite dead, Camille collapsed, and the police were sent for. When revived and questioned at length, Camille confessed—for she had no choice—that Hannah took a sleeping draught, and from there, things took a decidedly sour turn.

Was it chloral hydrate? Yes.

Was she in the habit of it? No.

So why last night? Camille pled ignorance.

By mid-morning, the police had everyone gathered in the parlor. All were subjected to private interviews, but none were interrogated so hard or so cruelly as Camille. No answer she gave seemed good enough, and since she was the only one with a key to the medicine chest, suspicion had only one direction in which to fall. And then it got worse.

"Where did you sleep last night?" the inspector asked.

"What business is that of yours?" Camille glared indignantly at him from her armchair. "I was in my bed, of course."

"Are you quite certain of that?"

Camille's gaze darted to the sheepish-looking maid who no doubt told all of what she saw, then back to the inspector. "What difference might it make where I slept?"

"Well, that depends." The inspector loomed over her. "Did you spend last night in the company of one of your girls?" He signaled for one of the uniformed policemen to bring a whimpering, sniffling Maddie forward.

Gasps echoed around the room.

"Yes." Camille winced. "But it's not what you imagine it to be." She began to wilt. "I've committed no crime. Maddie is of age, and I've done nothing against her will."

At that moment, one of the uniformed policemen returned from conducting a search of the bedrooms. He strode in bearing the fruits of his investigation: a half-empty bottle of brandy, two glasses, and a rubber priapus attached to two leather straps.

105

"What is this instrument of destruction?" The doctor homed in on the phallus, quick to spot the dried blood crusted around the crown. "This is how the damage was done!" Triumphant, he dragged Maddie to the center of the room and pointed a finger at Camille. "She has plied this young girl with alcohol and ruined the poor creature. What's gone on in this house is an abomination! I must insist that all the girls have their virtue checked at once."

He embarked on his crusade, and Camille put up no resistance. Why ought she? She had nothing to hide, and proved as much when his thorough inspections found no trace of any further wrongdoing.

When all was said and done—when Hannah's cold, stiff body had been removed to the mortuary, and the police departed to mull over their findings—Camille retired to her room with the remainder of the brandy and asked not to be disturbed. She refused lunch and dinner, and even Maddie's knock went unanswered. Not a sound was heard.

As evening turned into night, the frazzled matron ushered all the girls to their beds, but Maddie found decent sleep elusive. She tossed and turned for several hours before finally drifting into a fitful slumber, and when she woke at daybreak, it was to the distant echoes of a departing carriage and the faint but distinct scent of Camille's French perfume.

A familiar red satin ribbon was coiled on the bedside table, displayed on its side facing the bed, the words 'I love you' skillfully embroidered along it in pink silk thread. It was Camille's handiwork—she had no doubt of that—yet Camille was nowhere to be seen.

Consumed by a feeling of unease, she took the ribbon in her hand, slipped out of bed, and tiptoed down the hall. There was no light in Camille's room, but she rapped on the door anyway.

No answer.

She tried the handle, it opened freely, and she called out Camille's name.

Still nothing.

She pushed the door wide and cast her eyes upon the bed—the pristine, undisturbed bed— looking for any trace of Camille's existence.

There was none.

The armoire was open, nothing but bare hangers inside. There was no perfume on the vanity. No hairbrush, no hairpins, and no face powder, and her toothbrush was missing from the washstand.

Maddie clutched the ribbon in her fist and stormed over to the dresser, yanking drawers open at random, searching for evidence of Camille's intimates.

Empty.

Empty.

Empty.

Camille was gone.

Epilogue

A WEAK HEART WAS THE CAUSE. CAMILLE COULDN'T possibly have known—she bore no blame—but until the postmortem on Hannah was completed, much unflattering speculation and gossip circulated among the girls and the police. Had Camille dosed her too much? Had Camille sought to be rid of her? Had Camille done so because of her infatuation with Maddie? Is that why she ran away? Was she guilty?

In due course, parents and guardians were informed of events at the house and Maddie was among the first to be sent home. The doctor traveled with her and explained to her adoptive family at great length how she'd been robbed of her innocence, through no fault of her own. She was the victim. She was blameless. She was freed from all present marital obligations, for she was in no fit state to become a wife, and she happily played along.

There were tears aplenty. Much to her parents' dismay, she declared that she would never be able to give herself to any man after being violated in such a frightful manner. She'd been defiled. The trauma was unbearable. Entirely on account of the improper doings she was subjected to at Miss Harper's House of Etiquette, she was destined to be a spinster. Of course, to keep loneliness at bay, she surely needed to find herself a companion ...

Maddie made three laps around Leicester Square before summoning enough courage to enter the bawdyhouse she visited with Camille over a month ago. Worrying the ruffles in her silk dress, she ascended the back stairs and stepped into the sapphic haven. Some of the faces she remembered, others not. Many flashed her smiles, a few winked, but none caught her interest. She had a very specific taste.

Further into the main room, she spotted an older blonde sitting with an even older redhead and her heart leapt. The blonde's faultless figure was squeezed into a red silk evening gown, her décolletage bared. A pair of teardrop earrings dangled from her pierced ears, but she wore no other ornament. Her hair was pinned up too loosely to be respectable, and she crossed her legs at the knee.

"May I buy you a drink?" Maddie hovered over the blonde's shoulder.

"She's occupied," the redhead answered on her behalf. "Find yourself another."

"No other will do."

The blonde stopped breathing then. Her breath was trapped in her lungs, exhaled with a whisper when she turned to face the voice. "Maddie ..."

Camille's radiance was noticeably dulled. Her eyes had lost their luster, the dark circles beneath them barely obscured by the powder on her face. She was tired. In an attempt to bring life into her ashen cheeks, she'd applied her rouge too liberally. It would never pass for a natural blush, and her lips were no longer subtly pinkened with tinted beeswax, but daubed with bright crimson lip paste—a statement of her trade.

"Whatever she's paying you, I shall pay more." Maddie withdrew a crisp five pound note from her pocket, unsure of the proper etiquette. "Come home with me tonight, not a stranger."

Outbid and unwilling to compete, the redhead huffed and vacated the sofa while Camille stared at the note, one eyebrow arched, her jaw slack.

"I'm afraid you're overestimating my worth by some considerable degree." She clasped her hands around Maddie's to conceal the money, her nails chipped and cracked, the pearly coloring faded and neglected. "And I will not take so much as a penny from you in any case."

Maddie slid into the vacated spot beside her. "I both feared and hoped I'd find you here." She sat close. "Are you keeping well?"

"This life is not as easy for me as it once was." Camille adjusted her skirts, hiding a small ladder in her stockings above her ankle. "But I get by."

"Where've you been staying since you left the house?"

"Here and there." She hesitated to expound. "With whoever will take me."

"*I* will take you." Maddie pulled Camille's hands into her lap. "Not just for a night, but away from all of this rottenness for good." She peppered Camille's fingers with kisses. "I've recently become the recipient of a generous annuity. It will more than cover our expenses, and my parents need never know who you really are. You will be my companion. I shall say that I placed an advertisement in the newspaper, and that you were the most qualified applicant."

"An annuity?" Camille's brow creased. "From whom?"

"The Harper family." Maddie trailed her kisses up Camille's arm. "It appears they're rather keen for me to remain quiet about what went on when I was under their daughter's care, so I have enough money to keep you." Her kisses moved to Camille's neck. "If you'll let me."

Camille's face fell at the mention of Hannah. "I never meant to hurt her."

"You didn't," Maddie assured her. "Her heart gave out."

"Because I broke it."

"It wasn't your fault." Maddie pressed her lips to Camille's cheek. "We cannot help who we love, and I do love you so, so much."

"Your feelings haven't changed?"

"Not a bit."

"And what of the future?" Tears welled in Camille's eyes. "When I'm old and infirm?"

"I will love you still," Maddie swore. "I shall tend to your every need and sit by your bedside, reading you the bawdiest literature you like."

Camille chuckled, sending a few escaping tears tumbling down her cheeks. "You will make me a randy old woman."

"Randy and happy, I promise." Maddie pulled a hanky from her pocket. "Now dry your eyes and wipe off your lips. We have a train to catch."

ABOUT THE AUTHOR

Keira Michelle Telford is a multi-award-winning author with a love for the gruesome, the macabre, and the downright filthy. She writes dystopian science fiction, erotic lesbian romance, and other lesbian fiction.

<u>The SILVER Series</u>
www.ellacross.com

<u>The Prisonworld Trilogy</u>
www.carmenwild.com

<u>Erotic Lesbian Romance</u>
Cadence of My Heart
The Housemistress

<u>Other Titles</u>
Hoar & Rime (A Short Story)
Evonnia & the Maiden (A Short Story)

Website: www.keiramichelle.com
Facebook: www.facebook.com/keiramichelletelford
Goodreads: www.goodreads.com/keiramichelle
Amazon: www.amazon.com/author/keiramichelle

www.ingramcontent.com/pod-product-compliance
Lightning Source LLC
Chambersburg PA
CBHW070343130626
46556CB00007B/3011